THE SUTHERLAND DEVIL

CAROLINE LEE

ABOUT THIS BOOK

Everyone in the Highlands knows three things about the Sutherland laird:
1) He's got more bastards than he can count.
2) He's already buried three wives.
3) He's the very Devil himself.

Which is why, when Saffy—one of the Sinclair Jewels—finds evidence that her family's missing brooch is in the Sutherland Devil's possession, she's certain she's taking her life into her own hands to reclaim it. She's the scholar in the family, not the warrior...but how hard could it be to don a pair of braies, lop off her hair, and approach the Sutherlands as a lad?

She hadn't planned on being accused of spying and thrown into the dungeons to starve!

Merrick Sutherland is harried from all sides: his alliances are falling apart, his children are adorable monsters, and his illegitimate brother has declared war in an attempt to claim his title. The last thing he needs is a distraction in the form of a lippy little cross-dresser, but that's what he gets when he drags his new prisoner up from the dungeons. Is she a spy?

The best way to learn her secrets is to keep her close, so Merrick makes "Saf" his squire, without revealing what he's already learned.

Thrust into a sensual game of wits with her new master, Saffy is surprised to learn that what everyone knows about him isn't quite true. As his squire, she's in a prime position to search for the missing Sinclair jewels, and she's willing to go through the very Devil himself to find them.

But will she lose her heart in the process?

Warning: <u>Scorching hot Highlander</u> romance!

Want the scoop on new books? Join Caroline's Cohort, an exclusive reader group! Or sign up for my mailing list by texting "Caroline" to 42828 to get started!

Hilarious Scottish RomComs:
The Hots for Scots (8 books)
Highlander Ever After (3 books)
Bad in Plaid (6 books)
Second-Chance Manor (2 books)
Those Kilted Bastards (4 books)
Surprise! Dukes (5 books)

Steamy Scottish Historicals:
The Sinclair Jewels (4 books)
The Highland Angels (5 books)

Sensual Historical Westerns:
Black Aces (3 books)
Sunset Valley (3 books)
Everland Ever After (10 books)

The Sweet Cheyenne Quartet (6 books)

Sweet Contemporary Westerns
Quinn Valley Ranch (5 books)
River's End Ranch (14 books)
The Cowboys of Cauldron Valley (7 books)
The Calendar Girls' Ranch (6 books)

Click **here** to find a complete list of Caroline's books.

*Sign up for Caroline's Newsletter to receive exclusive content and freebies, as well as first dibs on her books! Or if newsletters aren't your thing, follow her on **Bookbub** for a quick, concise new release alert every time she publishes a book!*

PROLOGUE

THE SINCLAIR LAIRD WAS AILING, and his daughters could tell, despite his blustery attempts to hide it. He sat in the large chair in his solar, the same as always, but his face was pale, and his hands gripped the wooden arms, as if to keep them from shaking.

"Ye'll be married to the MacLeod lad, and that's the end of it! I'll hear no more arguing," he growled, glaring at the twins in front of him.

Unconsciously, Saffy plucked at the threads of her kirtle, glancing at her sister. Of the two of them, the middle of the Sinclair sisters, Citrine was far braver. Or mayhap, just more foolhardy. She stood now, her hands on her hips, her foot tapping as she frowned fiercely at her father.

"Nay, Da, I'll no' marry some *boy* when ye clearly need me here!"

Saffy did her best to hide her wince, knowing Dougal, the Sinclair commander, was watching stoically. Her twin never backed down from a confrontation, but Da clearly wasn't up to arguing. Besides, it's not as if they hadn't known this was coming. Da had already married off his oldest and youngest daughters. The twins were the only ones left.

Their father labored to pull himself forward, the glare he was sending Citrine reminding Saffy very much of his old self. "I do *no'* need ye here, girl! I'm yer laird and father, and if I say ye're to marry for the betterment of the clan, then ye'll do so!"

Citrine stomped her foot. Actually stomped her foot like a child, which just showed how much she'd lost control. "Da! Ye're ill! Ye cannae ask me—"

"'Tis naught," the older man said, looking exhausted as he sank back in his chair. "I'll be better in nae time." He cocked his head slightly, studying the two of them. "But ye're good daughters to worry so. I'll no' send ye away yet."

Behind him, Dougal made a noise of disapproval. Saffy's eyes flicked to the large man, who glared at the two of them with his arms folded across his chest. He was Da's right-hand man, and always had the Sinclairs' best interest in mind. But she couldn't remember him ever staring at her or one of her sisters with such disgust before.

Da might believe this illness was naught, but he lacked the strength to even glare at his commander. "Ye think I made the wrong decision, Dougal?" he asked mildly.

"Aye," came the growled response. "Ye coddle them. Citrine's duty is to strengthen the alliance with the MacLeods, and I'll be happy to be the one to drag her to her wedding, if ye cannae."

Saffy actually backed up a step at the threat in the man's voice. Since Da had started on this mission to see his daughters married, Dougal had been an enthusiastic supporter. Did he really care so much he'd *force* Citrine to go?

But where Saffy was cautious, Citrine was daring. She strode *toward* the desk. "Ye think ye could *drag me* somewhere?"

Dougal lowered his arms. "There's naught ye could do to stop me, lass."

Citrine was a fair hand with a sword and bow, but Dougal had been the one to teach her what she knew, and he was probably right. Saffy was already moving to pull her twin back when Da spoke.

"Enough." He winced as he rubbed his stomach, and all three of them turned to him in concern. The old man waved away their stares and pulled himself upright once more. "Citrine *will* marry, but when I say. She is a loyal Sinclair, a good daughter, and a proud Jewel. Aye?"

Citrine's shoulders heaved as she tried to calm her breathing, and the muscles in her jaw twitched. Saffy reached out to take her twin's hand, offering what support she could.

"Aye, Da," Citrine finally ground out. "I'll follow yer orders." Her glare moved to Dougal. "But no' yet."

When she turned to stalk out of the room, Saffy kept a tight hold on her hand, leaving herself no opportunity to curtsey or take her leave. But it didn't seem to matter, the door slammed shut behind them, and Citrine continued her angry walk until they reached their own chamber.

"Can ye believe that man?"

Saffy released her sister while she sank down on the big bed. She and Citrine used to share it with Agata and Pearl, until they'd been married only a short time ago.

"We expected this, Citrine," she said softly, part calming, part regretful.

Da hadn't mentioned anything about a marriage contract for *her*. While she wasn't sure if she really did want to go off to be some man's wife, the *not knowing* was worse. During the winter, Da had announced he'd be looking for marriage alliances for his four daughters, the Sinclair Jewels. Agata, the eldest, had already been married and widowed by then, but Da announced Pearl's contract first, to the Sutherland Devil.

The man was twice wee Pearl's age, and rumored to be cold-hearted and vicious, caring naught for the bastards he'd spawned from here to Edinburgh. It was no surprise Pearl—who, as the youngest of the Jewels, had the closest connection to the Sinclair clan—had refused the marriage contract and instead demanded to be allowed to take holy vows. Da had reluctantly agreed, and despite Dougal's insistence on escorting Pearl—the way he'd demanded to *escort* Citrine today—had assigned his most loyal bodyguard to the task.

Saffy nor her sisters knew exactly what happened on that adventure, but Pearl and the Sinclair Hound had returned very much in love, and were now married. In fact, judging from the number of times the two of them had slipped away to the loch, she could very well be carrying Da's first grandchild.

Then, even before Pearl had returned, Agata found her marriage contract with the Mackenzies. It had been a shock, since her intended was the brother of her first husband. But her most recent letter was glowing and full of love...and news about the sisters' quest.

Aye, Citrine was the one who was most devoted to finding out what had happened to the missing Sinclair jewels—the clan brooch which was said to grant power to the laird—but Agata had done her part. And as the scholar among them, Saffy was just as excited about the possibility of solving the ancient riddle as the news her twin would be married before her.

Although, it must be nice to be wanted.

Over by the window, Citrine had halted her angry pacing and stood with her fingers laced behind her head, staring out at the summer landscape. If Saffy was known as the scholar, and Agata the lady, and Pearl the helper...then Citrine was the firebrand.

And if she wasn't burning right now, then this was a smolder.

"Citrine?" Saffy prompted carefully, not sure if she wanted to know what her twin was thinking.

"I've bought us some time," Citrine said without turning, her tone speculative. "Da willnae send me away too soon, and I'll continue to fight against Dougal's attempts to send me away. But that means I *cannae* leave."

Saffy frowned. "Wait, ye *want* to go to MacLeod land?"

Citrine scoffed without turning. "I've no desire to marry the second or fourth or ninth son of a laird. My husband will be strong!"

"Aye, but strength is no' power."

"Spoken like someone who prefers scrolls to blades," Citrine quipped, turning just enough to smirk over her shoulder.

"Spoken like someone who cannae manage to get through an entire lesson without dropping her sword."

Chuckling at the reminder of Saffy's ineptness at sparring, Citrine lowered her hands to her hips. "Ye do well enough."

"No' nearly as well as *ye*." Her twin's prowess with a blade was well-known among the clan, and she often trained with the warriors, despite Dougal's irritation. Da never seemed interested in denying this particular fire-eyed Jewel anything. But the twins' differences weren't the point. "But ye said ye were no' able to leave at all? Do ye want to leave, then?"

"No' with him so sick!" Citrine threw herself down on the bench, sprawling in a way guaranteed to make Agata scold, were she there. "Da says it's naught, but he's no' one to sicken easily. And he's no' coughing or sneezing or fevered…it's his stomach."

Saffy nodded, having noticed the same thing. "But no one else is ill."

"Aye, so we cannae even blame tainted meat…"

Citrine's musings were distracting, and Saffy shook her

head as she steered her twin back on the right course. "So ye *willnae* be leaving?"

"One of us has to."

When Saffy met her sister's golden eyes, she understood. "The jewels."

"Aye," Citrine breathed.

After Pearl's departure, the remaining sisters had found a clue to the missing brooch: an ancient tapestry from their grandmother, given to their old nurse for safe-keeping. The tapestry had pointed them to Mackenzie land, where Agata was due to journey. She spent the first weeks of her marriage searching for another clue to the missing brooch, but ultimately found one of the jewels itself.

Saffy scrambled across the bed and reached beneath to pull out the small chest where they'd stored it. Her notes and scrolls were on the top, and beneath them was the carefully folded tapestry. She sat cross-legged on the coverlet and laid each pile around her, eager to reach the bottom of the chest and the only Sinclair jewel they had.

The large agate—nigh as big as her palm—was perfectly round and smooth, flecked with gold, just like Agata's eyes. Their oldest sister and her new husband had followed a clue in an old family saying, and discovered the jewel hidden inside a wooden map of the Highlands…under the space representing the Sutherland holding.

"Ye think one of us needs to go to the Sutherlands, do ye no'?" Saffy was sure that's what her twin meant, but needed confirmation.

"Well, Pearl cannae go!" Citrine threw her hands up in exasperation. "She's our wee sister—it's my job to protect her."

"Nay, 'tis Gregor's job now."

Citrine rolled her eyes. "Aye, ye're right. But she's no' part of this mission. She's a wife now, and likely to be a mother soon, judging from the moon-eyed looks the Hound keeps giving her. The Sutherland clue Agata sent was a *good* one."

But scary. Saffy swallowed. "Mayhap we should wait for her to finish her work with the map? She said she'd write again if she found aught else."

"Like the rest of the jewels?" Citrine shook her head before Saffy could answer. "They're no' there. Were they, she would have found them already." She leaned forward and propped her elbows on her knees. "The tapestry led us to the Mackenzies, where one jewel was hidden. The Mackenzie clue is pointing us to the Sutherlands. Ye ken I'm right, Saffy."

Staring down at the large stone in her palm, Saffy had to admit the truth. "Aye." She took a shuddering breath. "And that's no' all."

Her twin shifted, excitement evident in her voice. "Ye found something in the histories?"

Reluctantly, Saffy nodded and looked up, meeting Citrine's gaze. "Remember, our great-grandsire's second wife was a Campbell?"

"Aye, and so was the Mackenzie's ancestress!"

"They were sisters."

Citrine whistled long and low while she considered the information. "So *that* would explain how the jewel got to the Mackenzie holding!"

Saffy bit her lip, unsure if she should volunteer the rest of what she'd found, knowing it would be the final piece they needed. The clue which would send either her or Citrine to the Sutherland holding, where the devil himself held court.

"Saf?" her twin prompted. "What are ye no' saying?"

There was no hiding it. "They had another sister. Who married a Sutherland."

Citrine exploded off the bench in an excited flurry of limbs. "*Aye!*" she yelled, bouncing energetically and swinging an imaginary sword. "*That's it!*" She was grinning when she turned back to Saffy, breathing heavy. "Ye've found it! Agata's clue, the Mackenzie saying, the sister connection…" She threw herself onto the bed, grabbing one of Saffy's hands. "Ye've proven that the Sutherlands have the jewels!"

"Or mayhap just another clue on this chase," Saffy cautioned.

Her sister scoffed. "Even if 'tis just another of the jewels, 'twould be fine! Having *two* of the Sinclair jewels back in the keep would be worth it! Da would—"

When she bit down on her words, Saffy squeezed her hand, knowing what she had meant to say.

A clan legend said that with the brooch—the symbol of their power—missing, the Sinclair name was bound to fall. Leadership of the clan *could* pass to one of the Jewels, but it was rumored that Duncan having only daughters was proof the legend was coming true. There would be no strong sons to take over when Da died…or was too ill to carry on. The sisters suspected that's why he was so intent on marrying them off, so they'd be safe, but Citrine had never accepted it.

The legend also said that only the strongest and bravest of the Sinclair warriors would be able to restore the jewels and the clan's future, and Saffy had often privately wondered if *that* was why Citrine trained so hard. Would her husband be as accepting of her strange skills as the Sinclairs were? Hopefully, it wouldn't matter, because the jewels would be found and legend irrelevant by the time Citrine married.

With even *two* of the jewels back home, the legend would be proved wrong. The clan would know their future would be strong—whatever the future *did* hold—and that might be enough. And hopefully, their father's health would improve.

"I still think we should tell Da about the agate and the tapestry."

Citrine's response was swift. "Nay! I—" She shook her head and pulled her hand from Saffy's grip. "I dinnae ken how to say it. This illness of his is too convenient, too coincidental. I want…" She shrugged as she pulled herself into a cross-legged position, mirroring Saffy's. "I want to be *sure* afore we present him with what we've found."

"Ye think…what? That he's been cursed?" Saffy scoffed.

Citrine shrugged. "That, or poisoned."

Gasping, Saffy shook her head. "Dinnae even *hint* at that! Who would do such a thing?"

Her twin frowned, a determined look coming to her eyes. "I dinnae ken, but I'm going to find out."

Citrine couldn't leave the Sinclair holding, not yet at least. If she left now, Da would see no reason not to send her—and Dougal—to the MacLeods for her own unwanted wedding. And if she did, that would mean she'd be unable to keep a watch on Da's illness.

And if she couldn't leave, the clue to the Sutherlands would go unstudied.

All signs pointed to the Sutherlands having a jewel, or at least there being another clue at their holding. Relations between the Sinclairs and Sutherlands had been frosty since Da had been forced to call off the wedding between Pearl and the Devil who led the other clan, so they'd be unable to approach this problem diplomatically.

One of them would have to go there, to find a way to search the keep without giving away their mission. A disguise, mayhap, to ensure the Sutherland never discovered his once-fiancée's sister under his roof?

And Citrine couldn't do it, which left…

Saffy groaned and threw herself backward on the bed, hoping she wasn't making the biggest mistake of her life.

"I'll do it."

CHAPTER 1

"We've had no luck tracking him, milord. The slippery bastard must be moving his camp."

Merrick Sutherland, one of the most feared men in the Highlands, scowled down at his venison. It was prepared the way he preferred, and the wild onions were worth savoring. But it would've tasted better had it been accompanied by good news. Or at least silence.

"I was *sure* he was hiding in that valley," he muttered, not wanting the bairns to overhear the conversation. "'Twas the logical place, considering his raids of the last month."

His second, Gavin, grunted an acknowledgement as he sank to the bench across from Merrick and reached for a flagon. "But 'tis as I said. He might've been there, or thereabouts. If he moved before the rain we got two days ago, we'd have no way of kenning."

It was galling, not being out there with his men, searching for the bastard who'd been making life so difficult for the Sutherland. John Lindsay had always been a thorn in his side, believing he had a claim to Merrick's title…but he was only a nuisance until last year, when he'd surrounded himself with a band of his cursed, Lowlander kinsmen, and begun burning, reiving, and destroying Sutherland crops. His plan was clearly to draw Merrick out, to battle him directly, and as far as the laird was concerned, he'd oblige.

He'd be happy to kill the man himself, bastard brother or not. After all, it wouldn't be the first time, would it?

"Thomas says it's no' likely to rain again," Gavin offered helpfully. "Mayhap Lindsay's next raid will happen soon, and we can track him."

Merrick's hand, resting beside his trencher, clenched into a fist until his knuckles whitened. Aye, they'd find the bastard. They'd track him down, and Merrick would spill his blood as payment for the pain and destruction the man had wrought. Last summer, he'd been merely a nuisance, but even before the snow had melted this year, John Lindsay had begun his raids again. More than a few Sutherland farmers were homeless now, or hadn't been able to plant their crops. It was up to Merrick and his warriors to protect their clansmen, but they'd been unable to find the damned Lindsay.

Soon, he vowed.

"What happens if you cannae find him, Father?"

Merrick's gaze swung to Mary, sitting a few places down from him. "What?" he snapped, his scowl still in place.

His eldest never seemed to mind his dark moods. She shrugged daintily, the movement sending her brown curls swinging. Since her best friend Elana—Gavin's younger sister, who worked in the kitchens—had gone south to visit family, Merrick noticed his daughter was paying more attention to her hair and clothing choices.

Or mayhap that had nothing to do with Elana…

Mary smiled peacefully. "If ye dinnae track Lindsay, Da, do yer warriors just have to wait—"

"We'll find him." Merrick's tone brooked no argument.

"Aye, Lady Mary," young Andrew hastened to add. "If yer

father says we'll do something, we'll do it. Have some more venison, please."

The lad had been Merrick's squire for years, and only now risen to the rank of warrior. At eighteen—a year older than Mary—he was obviously proud to be seated with his laird's inner circle, but Merrick's frown deepened when he saw how solicitous the lad was being to Mary. And damn if Mary wasn't blushing. He vowed to sit Andrew on his other side tomorrow, away from his daughter.

Hell, this is what I'm reduced to planning these days?

God willing, Gavin's men would soon have a trail, and Merrick would be able to actually do something useful instead of sitting here in the keep, worrying about his daughter's virtue like an old woman.

I'm no' ready to be a grandda.

Gavin distracted him by muttering, "She's right, ye ken. With Lindsay's raids, we'll be stretched thin. Now that Mackenzie's married one of the Sinclair Jewels, we'll have to contend with both of them, and can ill afford—"

"Is there a reason ye think I dinnae ken this?" Merrick snapped, his appetite waning by the second. "A reason ye think I need ye to explain it all to me?"

The Sinclairs were a powerful ally, and he'd known Duncan Sinclair for years. Making a marriage alliance with one of the man's daughters had been common sense, although Merrick had dragged his feet, not wanting to bother with another wife. But then Duncan himself had broken the engagement when his daughter had married a common warrior from his own clan. It had been a bit of a relief, honestly, up until the Mackenzie's regent had married one of Duncan's other daughters. Now, he had to contend with united power on either side of his borders, while Lindsay made their lives miserable within his lands.

If Mackenzie chose to attack anytime soon, with the

Sutherland warriors already having so much to do, they'd be in trouble. But Merrick would never let his men see he was concerned. He held Gavin's gaze long enough for the man to lower his chin in submission.

"Aye, milord," Gavin said quietly and reached for the haunch of meat on his trencher.

Blowing out a breath, Merrick slumped back in his chair and allowed his fist—and the rest of his muscles—to relax. He knew he was defensive because he was frustrated at being unable to find Lindsay. But he'd never been any good at hiding his bad moods.

It was why he was called Devil, after all.

At that moment, a commotion broke out from the end of the table where the rest of the children sat. Merrick blinked, his brooding interrupted.

"Beck!" screeched nine-year-old Adelaide. "How could ye?" The girl stood, a splotch of gravy spreading across her kirtle.

His gaze flicked to the bairn's nurse, old Nell, who was whispering urgently to six-year-old Beck, the wildest of them all. The lad didn't look at all repentant. In fact, he was already reaching for another onion, obviously intent on firing another volley at his sister.

But before he could, eight-year-old Eva shot to her feet, a roll in her hand. "Ye have the manners of a *pig*!" She screeched as she lobbed the bread across the table.

Of course, Beck took that as an opening, and flicked the onion in her direction. Honestly, the lad had remarkable aim, which meant that since he hit Nolan, he'd probably planned to do it. But Nolan was as stoic as Eva was wild, and just grunted as he continued to eat. In fact, the sturdy lad picked up the onion which had bounced off his shoulder and popped it into his mouth.

Eva screeched louder in offense, reaching for a piece of cheese. Little Isobel began to bounce up and down in Nell's lap, laughing and clapping, while twelve-year-old Maggie scooped up her knife and leapt to her younger brother's rescue.

In a matter of moments, chaos reigned. Merrick pinched the bridge of his nose, wondering if this was normal. Did other powerful lairds have to put up with this amount of disorder at their supper tables? Or was it just his luck, with so many bairns?

He waited for Nell to get the lot of them under control, but the old woman had her hands full with three-year-old Isobel. Not only that, but baby Emma had woken and began wailing in her basket, so Nell was trying to quiet the wee thing.

It didn't help that Merrick's men had immediately began calling out encouragement, and in some cases, taking bets on which of his unruly offspring would prevail. Most of them had a soft spot for Maggie and Beck, who spent their time watching the men train and mimicking their techniques. But Eva was fierce, and lacked Adelaide and Mary's control, and Merrick heard more than one of his men refer to her as "Wee Lightening."

Chaos. Utter chaos.

And despite his earlier mood, Merrick felt a smile tug at his lips as he slouched in his chair, watching his children throw food at one another gleefully.

Any moment now, he'd put an end to this, he vowed. Any moment…

Isobel was trying to climb off Nell's lap and reach for a chunk of the thick, brown bread, while Maggie used Beck's trencher as a shield. Of course, this meant their supper had spilled all over the table in front of them, but at least she was protecting the lad as he fired missiles at his older siblings. They made a good team.

Eva was screaming insults, lobbing food back across the table, while Nolan ignored most of them. When he finished his own venison, he reached for his sister's—maybe there was a reason the lad was so stocky. Bookish Adelaide appeared close to tears as she lectured her siblings at the top of her lungs, and Mary huddled close to Andrew, while the young man gallantly shielded her.

Merrick's smile slipped away at that sight.

Definitely time to separate those two.

Mayhap Beck felt similarly, because he switched his aim to his eldest sister, flicking onions in her direction in between ducking Eva's volleys. Andrew was doing a damn good job of batting the missiles out of the air, Gavin was roaring with laughter, and Merrick shook his head in exasperation.

Mackenzie breathing down my neck, Lindsay raiding my lands, and my own children are no better than a lawless band of reivers themselves.

Still, at least it kept the meal from being boring.

Time to put an end to this. He sat forward abruptly, ready to roar his irritation—mayhap a trifle more feigned than real, in order to show the bairns he was serious. And he would've, except at that moment, an onion sailed out from behind Beck's trencher, headed not for Mary or Eva, but Merrick himself.

He hadn't spent over a decade as the Sutherland laird with poor reflexes. Before the gooey orb could connect with his shoulder, Merrick snatched it out of the air.

Instantly, silence descended. Every one of his unruly offspring, every man in the great hall, immediately ceased their raucous noise and watched him warily. Only baby Emma hadn't seemed to notice the interruption—her wails continued unabated while Nell watched her laird with an open mouth.

Sure, he had their attention; Merrick held Beck's gaze and slowly squeezed the onion until he felt it pop and the juices flow between his fingers. It was satisfying, to find a way to release some of his earlier irritation. But not enough.

"Beck," he growled.

His son swallowed audibly. "Yes, milord?"

"Come. Here."

It was almost comical the way the lad scrambled away from the table. Beside him, Maggie sat down heavily, her guilty gaze on him, as if wondering if she would be punished. Eva stood defiantly, her shoulders heaving with exertion, while tears of frustration dried on Adelaide's cheeks.

Every present clan member watched as Beck shuffled around the table to reach his father. As he passed Mary, the girl leaned away from him, and for the first time, Merrick noticed Andrew had his arm around her back. But he didn't have time to react before his troublesome son stood before him.

Merrick shifted in his large chair until he was glaring directly at the six-year-old, who met his gaze bravely. The lad's blond hair was dotted with breadcrumbs from a volley Maggie hadn't been able to block in time, but he managed to look unrepentant.

And—despite Merrick's fierce glower, he could admit the truth—damn cute. Had Willie looked like that at six? It was hard to remember. Merrick was certain *he'd* never been so cherubic, but Robbie probably had. Robbie had always looked so innocent.

The knowledge Beck might one day follow Robbie's path leant anger to Merrick's scowl. Without speaking, he reached out and wiped his oniony hand on the lad's shoulder, smearing the gravy and onion juice across Beck's shirt, so he matched Adelaide.

And the boy, damn his eyes, lowered himself into a courtier's flourishing bow. "Thank ye, milord," he breathed reverently, as if Merrick had knighted him.

Around them, his men began to murmur, and Merrick heard a few chuckles at his son's impertinence. Even while he himself was battling the urge to smile at the lad's attitude, he knew he couldn't become the clan's laughingstock. He commanded his men with absolute certainty and was respected for it. His children would feel the same, by God.

"Beck," he growled, "If ye make it to manhood, ye will have to ken respect. Yer commander will demand it, and ye *will* start now, by showing yer laird and father what is deserved."

Apparently his tone got through to the little hellion, because Beck's expression immediately sobered, and he hunched his shoulders as he dropped his gaze to Merrick's chin. "Aye, Father," he whispered.

"Ye disrespect yer nurse and yer sisters by acting as ye did, and ye disrespect me."

Beck swallowed again. "I'm sorry, milord. I only meant to lighten the mood."

Merrick allowed the silence to stretch just long enough for Gavin across the table to shift uncomfortably, before he nodded to release the tension. "Apology accepted." But before the lad could breathe a sigh of relief, he continued, "Ye've made a mess, lad." Merrick nodded at the woven cloth covering the table, now splattered with venison and gravy from Beck's trencher. "Ye, Maggie, and Eva will have no more meals until ye scrub this cloth and Adelaide's kirtle. One of the scullery lasses will no doubt show ye what needs to be done."

Beck's brown eyes flashed toward Maggie, who was looking livid at what she no doubt saw as servant's work. Eva was whispering furiously to Nolan, who was ignoring her. But Beck just nodded slowly.

"Aye, milord."

Merrick liked that the boy accepted his punishment without whining or arguing. He clasped the six-year-old on his shoulder. "Remember this, lad. A real warrior takes what is meted out with grace and determination to do better."

Beck nodded, chewing on his lower lip. Under Merrick's

hold and gaze, the lad shifted on his feet. Was he aware that most of the Sutherlands in the room were watching him now? Was he embarrassed? Good. That would go further toward teaching him restraint than anything else, likely.

For his part, Merrick was pleased he wouldn't have to exert his control any further. He didn't want to break this mischievous boy any more than he wanted Mary snuggling up with his former squire. But he would *not* allow his power to be doubted, not in his own great hall.

John Lindsay, his own brother, was already pulling this clan apart. Merrick would not allow his control to be questioned, not by a six-year-old, and not by the men watching what was happening.

He would remain strong. In command. And if that meant having the reputation of the Devil himself, so be it.

"Well, lad?" he asked quietly. "Is there aught else you need to say to your laird?"

"Aye," Beck whispered, his hands twisted in front of him.

Merrick waited a moment, but the boy didn't seem inclined to continue. He hated the thought that he might've crushed Beck's spirit, but it had to be done if he wanted his men to know *he* was strong.

"Beck?" he prompted, and squeezed the boy's shoulder just a bit. "What would you say to your laird?"

That's when the lad looked up, and his dark eyes met Merrick's. "I love ye, Da," he whispered just before he threw himself toward Merrick.

The man grunted just slightly when the boy slammed into his chest and wrapped his small arms around his middle. Then, accepting the inevitable, Merrick released his breath through his teeth, and tightened his hold on the lad, in something akin to a hug.

"Aye, lad," he murmured against the mop of blond curls. "I love ye, too."

It was the truth. No matter how much the lad reminded him of Robbie, no matter that he was going to drive Merrick mad with his antics and the way he incited chaos among his siblings, Merrick loved him.

Him, and every single one of the bairns now staring at them with expressions ranging from irritation to smugness to anticipation.

Even the Devil could love his children, aye? Although God help him if the word got out.

He looked across the table and met Gavin's eyes a moment before the other man lifted his flagon to his lips and looked away. Merrick found himself growling a warning.

"No' a word."

Gavin's brows twitched, which told the laird his friend *wanted* to say something, but wouldn't. His second had been with him since they'd both been lads, being a few years younger than Merrick. He was lucky to have Gavin's support, and knew the commander would keep his secret.

A cry from outside had Gavin's head snapping up, the same as Merrick's and half the men in the hall. Even young Andrew straightened away from Mary, already looking toward the main doors. Gently, Merrick set Beck away from him—the lad rushed to his oldest sister's arms—and slowly stood.

The doors burst open, and Daniel flung himself into the room, his face red, and his expression excited. "Lindsay, milord! He's hit the croft at the bend in the river!"

"How long ago?" Merrick growled, forcing down the burst of satisfaction until he was sure.

"Just now! Murray's eldest rushed to report."

Slowly, Merrick's lips curved upward. It wasn't a nice smile, but his men erupted in cheers anyhow. "We have him, lads," he called.

In a flurry of movement, the Sutherland warriors abandoned their meals and rushed for the stables, their laird among them. Merrick glanced back toward the bairns only once, to see them all watching with wide eyes. He nodded to let them know everything would be fine, then met Andrew's eyes.

His former squire still stood by the bench beside Mary, obviously torn. Had he been anyone else, Merrick would've disciplined him for putting a woman before his duty to his laird. But the lad had only recently joined the ranks of warriors, and while he was used to remaining at Merrick's side, he knew he wasn't seasoned.

So, Merrick pointed a finger at him. "You will guard my family and this keep. If aught happens, if any of them come to harm, you will pay. Understood?"

The dark-haired lad seemed relieved to have the decision made for him. He clasped his fist to his chest and lowered his head in acceptance. "I will guard them as if they were my own."

Probably exactly what he wanted. Merrick resisted the urge to sniff sarcastically. Instead, he narrowed his eyes. "My family will be your charge until I say otherwise."

"*Without fear!*" the lad shouted, and the clan motto was repeated by the few men who hadn't left the hall already.

Merrick nodded. "Without fear," he confirmed, then strode out, having already put Andrew—and the bairns—from his mind. He had a job.

Brother or not, John Lindsay would be caught. Caught and punished like the dog he was.

The Sutherland Devil's blood began to pump in anticipation.

CHAPTER 2

THE SHORELINE of the small loch looked empty, but a fortnight of caution wasn't easy to overlook. Saffy waited in the shadows at the edge of the forest, scanning the beach and the distant water.

No one. She was safe.

Still, her senses were on high alert as she scuttled from the safety of the trees to the water. While her disguise should be sufficient to fool any passersby, it'd be easier to just avoid as many people as possible, as she'd been doing. But her thirst was strong enough to conquer her fear of being seen.

She kicked off her shoes and crouched in the shallows, not caring her stockings were getting wet. Nay, with the heat and the sweat drying under her linen shirt, she welcomed the way the cold water felt against her skin.

In fact, before she could scoop up some of the water to drink, she gave up on propriety and just knelt in the water, sighing a bit in relief. Her small sword bumped against her heels, but she shifted it out of the way so she could cup a handful of water.

It was cold and clear, everything she could've hoped for.

She drank until she thought her stomach might burst. After surviving on berries and nuts and two stolen loaves, she was ready to do just about *anything* for a haunch of meat and a cup of ale. She'd even blunder her way through another lecture and practice session with Citrine!

Thirst quenched, Saffy braced her palms against the rocky bottom and stared down at her reflection in the water. Ripples marred the surface, but the sun was bright enough for her to see the mess she'd made of herself. The scrapes and scratches across her forehead and cheeks came from traveling and hiding from sight in brambles, but most were hidden by the chopped locks of hair which half-obscured her vision.

All of the Sinclair Jewels had the same dark blonde hair, and although Saffy was by far the most scholarly of her sisters, she'd always taken great pride in her hair. It seemed sad that now, not only was it cut as short as a lad's, but *she'd* been the one to do it.

When Munro had left her in Dornach and returned home, certain she was there for a visit and well-guarded, she'd stayed only long enough to change into lad's clothing Citrine had acquired, and tuck her hair up under a *chaperon* hood. Then she'd snuck out, and once safe in the woods, grasped her hair in one fist, her knife in the other, closed her eyes, and done a poor job of chopping it all off.

Still, it had felt...*liberating* somehow, to be dressed as a lad and traveling alone. Is this how Citrine felt all the time? She didn't wear a disguise, of course, but she was always so intent on standing on her own feet and learning to protect herself. Her sister should be the one on this adventure, but Saffy knew her twin was needed at home, to watch over Da. It was scary to realize Citrine would have no way of contacting her, and Saffy wouldn't be able to write home until this adventure was complete. They'd agreed that any attempt her twin made to contact the Sutherlands would only raise suspicion, so when they'd hugged goodbye that last time, it had felt frighteningly *final.*

Citrine had been the one to fetch this disguise and give Saffy the small sword which now hung on her belt. She almost wished her sister could see their handiwork now.

Saffy stared down at her reflection. Besides the wet stockings, she wore a set of braies, which were more comfortable than she'd suspected, and a lad's belted surcoat over a linen shirt. It wasn't a common costume here in the Highlands, where most of the Sinclair menfolk wore their kilts in the summer heat, but she hadn't questioned Citrine's choices. The surcoat was sleeveless, so not *too* warm, and hid her breasts. Of course, she'd tied them down the way her twin had shown her, and they'd both giggled at the thought that the precaution they used while training could be useful as a disguise.

And although Saffy had never considered herself vain, as she stared at her reflection, she had to admit it was a little disconcerting how easy it was for her to turn into a lad.

She sighed and pushed herself to her feet once more, glad she felt better. There was still several hours of daylight left, and she guessed she'd be close to the Sutherland stronghold soon.

Over the last sennight, she'd discovered strength she hadn't known she possessed. Her feet ached and her legs were tired, but she would push on. It was the lack of sleep—curled up on the hard ground, starting at every noise, waiting for dawn—which was wearing her down. If she didn't reach the Sutherland keep soon, didn't find a place to rest, she wasn't sure how much longer she'd be able to travel like this.

As she walked, she stripped berries from bushes and shoved tubers in her pouch for later. Who would've thought that treatises on the natural bounties of the land would come in handy this way? Definitely not Saffy, curled up safely in the window seat of Da's solar all those years ago. That was also where she'd studied and memorized the maps which she now followed unerringly, and where she'd heard the stories of the Sutherland Devil.

The laird had been friends with Da when they were both younger. A decade ago, the man had hanged a lad for thieving. Da had cut him down at the last moment, and Gregor, half-dead and grateful, had pledged himself to the Sinclairs, and become the Sinclair Hound. Although few people knew the whole story, Pearl had told her sisters after her wedding to Gregor.

It was just one more example of Merrick Sutherland's fierceness.

Despite the sun beating down overhead, Saffy shivered at the thought of having to meet the man on his own land. Of course, God willing, she'd never have to set eyes on him. Her plan, carefully constructed with Citrine, was to infiltrate the Sutherland keep as a serving lad. Or mayhap find work in the stable—although she had no experience with horses, at least she'd be further away from the laird and possible detection. She'd *prefer* to find work with the clan's priest or seneschal, anywhere she could serve as a scribe...but such a position would mean a greater likelihood of meeting the laird, which was *not* her goal.

Back home, Citrine had vowed to do her best to cover for her absence. She'd been the one to talk Munro—one of Da's warriors—into accompanying Saffy as far as the abbey Dornach. Hopefully, Da and Dougal would think Saffy was safely visiting the abbey, studying the scrolls and holy writs in the library there, which had happened twice before.

Which meant she had a few weeks, at most, before someone would get suspicious about her lack of contact. In that time, she needed to search the Sutherland keep, find whatever evidence she could of the missing Sinclair jewels, and make her way back home.

All without allowing the Sutherland Devil to know of her mission.

If one—or all—of the missing stones were on Sutherland land, as the sisters suspected, then would the laird be considered culpable? Would that anger him, to know he'd harbored stolen jewels for so long? Or was he part of the plot against the Sinclairs, intent on keeping his old friend weak, knowing Duncan Sinclair's line would fail?

Nay, better to hide her intent from the Sutherlands. Better to hide *herself* from the laird.

As the sun sank lower in the west, Saffy began to think about making camp. Although, with the way her nights had been going, it'd be better to push herself as far as possible, then make a small fire once the dark truly set in. The further she went today, the closer she'd be to her goal.

But God forgive her, she was *tired*. Hours and hours and hours of fear and caution and tenseness had brought her to this point. All of her limbs felt heavier, and she caught herself stumbling once or twice.

Mayhap she *should* halt her travels. If she was this tired, mayhap she'd finally sleep well?

She pushed out of the woods, heading towards the distant sparkle of a loch below her. The path was easy, and she knew she wasn't more than a few hours walk from her destination now. She could drink, make camp, *sleep*…then tomorrow, mayhap well-rested, she could set her mind toward finding a way into the good graces of whoever was in charge of hiring at the Sutherland keep.

It wasn't until the third time she stumbled over the rocks in the path that she realized how dull her mind really was. She was looking, but not *seeing*. She'd pushed out of the cover of the forest without even searching the landscape for danger.

Which is why, when she finally heard the hoofbeats, there was no place to hide. Saffy stood, her mind dazed from exhaustion, as the men on horseback surrounded her. Dimly, she reached for her sword, but her hands fumbled on the simple steps required to remove it from the scabbard.

"I'll cut ye down where ye stand, brigand!"

The man who yelled had leveled a heavy sword at her as his horse pranced in place. Saffy squinted, trying to make sense of what she was seeing. He was little more than a lad, probably only a few years younger than herself. And he wore the Sutherland plaid. In fact, *all* the men wore it.

"I—I am no brigand." Her voice was rough, scratchy with exhaustion and fear, although part of her mind was pleased it disguised her sex even further.

With the sword, the lad gestured to her clothing. "Ye're a Lindsay, are ye no'?"

A Lindsay? They were a Lowland clan, and her clothing marked her as an outsider. It would make sense to claim to be from a clan *other* than the Sinclairs…but if the Lindsays were met with this kind of welcome, mayhap not.

Mutely, she shook her head.

The lad laughed, his sword never wavering, even as his horse stepped impatiently. "Ye think me a clot-heid? John Lindsay and his men have been raiding for months, and were just sighted today. Obviously, they've led our laird on a chase away from the keep, while sending *ye* to infiltrate our home!"

Enraged now, the lad slid from his horse and stalked toward her. Dimly, she noted he had fine features, russet hair in the same cropped style she now wore. But it was hard to be appreciative when he swung the sword so that it stopped above her shoulder, entirely too near her neck.

When she flinched away, all she could manage in her current exhausted state, his lips curved cruelly. "What was your plan, lad? Ye think ye could get close to us, because ye're so young?" He spat in disgust, then shook his head. "My laird left me in charge of guarding his family, and I'll die before I allow you near them."

She shook her head once more, although the movement was stilted, with the sword so close. "I'm no' a brigand," she managed again.

He leaned closer. "As far as I'm concerned, *all* Lindsays are brigands, for daring to support that bastard."

What bast— Oh, he must mean John Lindsay. Her normally quick mind was sluggish, trying to understand what he meant. When the sword twitched once more, she gave up trying to understand and focused on the very real chance she was about to be killed by a lad younger than her.

From behind her, an elderly voice asked, "What will ye do, Andrew?"

Andrew tensed, bringing the edge of the sword against her throat. She felt a sting, but dared not flinch, for fear of sending the blade deeper. Her eyes widened with fear as she felt blood trickle down her neck. Part of her noted this group of men must've been those left behind to guard the keep—the very old and a lad like Andrew—but it didn't seem to matter right now.

Should she reveal her identity? Would it help her or hurt her in this instance?

Well, it would ruin *everything*, but it was—as Citrine would say—a hell of a lot better than dying. Especially being killed for being a Lindsay brigand.

She'd opened her mouth to blurt out her secret, when suddenly, Andrew exhaled and stepped back.

He was still glaring at her when he said, "The Sutherland would have my head if I didn't allow him to question the lad. He's young, but if he was sent to infiltrate our home, sent to cause God kens what kind of havoc, then he must ken *something* of that bastard's plans."

She wasn't going to die today?

"The dungeon, then?" the unseen voice called out.

Andrew's nod was more of a jerk. "Aye. A few days without food and water, and the lad will be ready to spill *all* his secrets, even before the Sutherland starts his interrogation. Tie him up."

Interrogation.

A cold spike of fear punched through Saffy's daze at the thought of being at the Sutherland Devil's mercy. What kind of *interrogation* techniques would he use? He was rumored to be ruthless. And God help her if he found out she was a *woman*! His dead wives and many mistresses would likely attest to the fact the laird would treat a woman no differently than a man he suspected of betrayal.

The fear of being at his mercy had her heart pounding, and her breaths coming in pants. It was long moments before she realized her hands had been tied, her sword and knife taken, and she was being led behind Andrew's horse.

Her head hung as she stumbled along, pinned on all sides by horses and Sutherland men. She might've made a bid for freedom, trying to tug the rope out of Andrew's hands, but he had it wrapped tightly in his hand. And being so tired, she braced herself against the animal's haunches more than once to keep from falling.

By the time she caught sight of the Sutherland keep, her stomach had long since given up growling. Large, gray, and imposing—like the Devil who commanded it, she was sure—it sat high and proud, with plenty of space beneath for the dungeons.

Those dungeons—and the promised *interrogation*—so occupied her mind, she barely noticed the jeers from the gathered clan when Andrew announced they'd captured a Lindsay spy. Someone threw mud at her, but she was too dirty and tired—mentally and physically—to do more than duck her head.

The chaos was so overwhelming, it was almost a relief to be thrown into a deep pit of stone below the kitchens.

Almost.

Her cell was large, and she was the only occupant. When Andrew slammed the door shut, she huddled on the pile of dirty straw where she'd fallen, and wished for the strength to beat on the door.

It might be hopeless, to demand her release, but at least it'd be better than giving up.

But instead, she sat there, her knees drawn up to her chin, staring at the heavy door, doing naught but breathing and shivering. Vaguely, she knew she was in shock, but it was long moments before she could control her panic enough to concentrate on her breathing, and even longer before she could relax into a cross-legged position.

Even that movement wore her out.

She squeezed her eyes shut and forced herself to consider her advantages…

A locked cell without food or water.

No' an advantage.

A vengeful laird returning "in a few days", according to Andrew.

Definitely no' an advantage.

A bone-deep weariness, an aching thirst, and an empty belly.

Her eyes flew open in irritation.

Ye're no' verra good at this, Sapphire Sinclair.

A few days in this cell, starving, dying of thirst—

Stop!

She shoved herself to her feet, stumbling so hard she had to thrust out a hand to stop herself from falling over again. Of course, that might be a blessing if she knocked her head and managed to stop thinking such horrible thoughts.

She stood, panting, one palm flat against the stone beside

her, forcing herself to concentrate on her surroundings to distract from her looming starvation. There were two windows high in the walls—well above her head—through which a dim twilight filtered.

I suppose I should be thankful I'm no' in the dark.

That would be nice. She'd be able to *see* while she starved to death.

"God's wounds, Saf," she muttered to herself, shaking her head, and peering around the cell. Mayhap it had been a storage cellar at some point, and there was something useful for her.

In a depressingly short amount of time, she concluded her hope was in vain. Her cell was empty and bleak, complete with carvings from past prisoners.

Well, at least I willnae be bored.

It looked as if most of the carvings had been done by one hand, misspelled Latin phrases ranging from philosophical to lewd. But there was one…

She stumbled to the far wall. There, right in the middle, at head-height, was a deep carving of a sunburst, and a Latin phrase: *I shine, not burn.* Her fingers shook as they traced the lines in the quickly fading light. The sun had been carved across several stones which made up the wall, there was something ominous about it. Had the same prisoner carved this? How many days had he spent laboring over such a piece of art, and why? The phrase was oddly hopeful for someone confined to a dungeon cell…unless he'd been expecting to be burned at the stake?

Suddenly, she wanted nothing to do with such an image, hating it for reminding her of her doom. She *would* burn when the Sutherland returned.

That's what the Devil did, after all. Burned souls in hell.

Shivering once more—although from genuine cold now, rather than fear—she kicked the straw into a flimsy pile and sank down onto it. Wrapping her arms around her middle, she rested her head against the stone and stared at the carvings around her.

Assets:

Ye're where ye wanted to be.

She snorted, but couldn't help the way her lips tugged upward. Aye, she was deep in the Sutherland holding, but not at all free to look for her family's lost jewels.

Ye might finally get a good night's sleep.

That *was* something to look forward to. If she was already in as much danger as she could possibly imagine, then mayhap her mind would finally let her rest?

Ye willnae be bored.

Oh, aye.

Think of it this way: Ye might starve to death before the Sutherland returns to interrogate ye.

As she closed her eyes in despair, tears of exhaustion leaking from under her lids, she had to admit the truth:

Sometimes she really *hated* her mind.

CHAPTER 3

MERRICK'S MOOD was dark enough that his men had avoided him for the last two days.

Yesterday morning it had become clear they wouldn't be able to hunt down Lindsay or his followers. Still, he pushed his men, especially Gavin, to find some sort of trace of the reivers.

Murray's croft had been burned and his livestock slaughtered. Lindsay's insult was that he hadn't even bothered to steal the cattle. Any Highlander worth his salt had done his share of reiving from neighboring clans and understood the benefit of leaving the farm profitable enough to rob again. Aye, driving off cattle for their own gain would've been logical, but killing them was pure evil.

The crofter and his family were alive, thank God, and Merrick had left two of his men to help salvage what they could, then help Murphy's family return to the keep for protection. If these raids kept up, Merrick might have to consider moving more families to the safety of the village, even if the planting season was high and they'd miss valuable time in the fields.

Despite his earlier claims, Gavin had been unable to track Lindsay's men beyond the valley cairn. Their tracks didn't emerge anywhere the Sutherlands could find, which meant the wily bastard had escaped again.

When he'd accepted the inevitable, Merrick led his band of warriors back toward the keep, and pushed them hard.

Now, seeing his home looming above the village, he breathed a silent prayer of thanksgiving Lindsay hadn't manage to attack during his absence. The bairns were safe. His people were safe.

And his mood was still foul.

As they thundered into the courtyard, stable lads came running to take their animals. Some of his warriors had peeled off from the column on their way in, checking on their own homes and families. Those left either lived in the barracks or would make their way home on their own time.

For Merrick's part, he was already thinking about a hearty meal. He might've been livid at their failure, but he could no longer deny his hunger. The last meal had been oat cakes eaten on horseback, and he wondered what the cook, Corra, was preparing for supper.

"Father!"

Despite his mood, Merrick felt his heart lighten at the sight of Mary hurtling down the front steps toward him. Just as she'd done since she was a little girl, she threw herself at him, wrapping her arms around his waist, and burrowing her face into his chest.

"I'm glad you're safe," she murmured.

He was rank, and he knew it, but his daughter didn't seem to mind the smell of horse, sweat, and irritation. So, he shifted his sword and wrapped one arm around her. "Aye, it'll take more than a wee scourge like Lindsay to bring this auld man low."

"Ye're no' so auld!"

Mary chuckled as she straightened to grin up at him, and the sight caused his voice to stick in his throat. She looked so much like her mother when she smiled, and the memory was always bittersweet. Anna had been gone for—what?—nigh fifteen years now. He remembered little of her, except her smile, her zest for life, and the way he'd loved her.

But he had Mary and Willie, at least, to remind him of her.

How had the lad grown so much in the last year? Willie was a bastard, like his sister, but as his oldest son, he had power. So when Lindsay's raids had become more than a mere nuisance, Merrick had sent him to the MacDonnell to foster. And despite the danger, he missed the lad, just as he knew Mary and the rest of them missed him.

"Da?" Mary poked him in the side. "Ye look lost."

He shook his head, but knew his scowl was exaggerated when he glared at her. "A laird has many things on his mind, wee one."

Under his arm, she shrugged. "I take it yer hunt did nae go well?"

"Ye leave the warriors to worry about such things." He turned them both toward the steps, ready for a wash and some food. "How did things fare here in our absence?" He meant *How did Andrew do*, but he wouldn't ask his daughter's opinion of the lad so openly.

Apparently, he hadn't needed to. Mary beamed up at him, even as she lifted her skirts in one hand to climb the steps. "Andrew protected us all! He's such a fine warrior, Father, braw and smart and ever so handsome and—"

He cut her off, not wanting to hear his daughter list the lad's *other* features. "I'm glad ye're all safe. Any new bairns?"

Mary giggled as he pulled open the thick oak doors. "Nay, no' this time."

He pretended to sigh. "Mayhap next time."

Her laughter brought a smile to his face as well. It had been a joke between them. It was no secret how irritated he'd been when little Isobel had shown up several years ago. Beck had been barely four, and already running wilder than Nell could manage. Mayhap that's why Isobel's mother had waited to deliver the babe until Merrick had been away from the keep.

When he'd returned and been presented with a new daughter, his first words had been a snapped, "God's wounds, *another one?*"

But holding the wee cherub, staring down into serious brown eyes, he'd known the truth: he'd accept her, just as he'd accepted every other of his illegitimate children who'd made their way to him.

Devil he may be, but he knew his duty.

The tradition had risen then, of asking Mary about new bairns when he returned to the keep. It'd been right after Hogmany—his visit to the Sinclairs to arrange that failed marriage alliance, in fact—when he'd returned to the news of baby Emma's arrival. The wee bairn's mother had died soon after delivery, and Mary herself had named the tiny thing.

His sarcasm had made Mary chuckle, and he basked in the sound.

The great hall seemed no different than when he'd left. He released his hold on her shoulder and stepped back, peering into the corners. "Beck didnae burn aught down while I was gone?"

"Nay, Father," Mary giggled. "And Maggie only smuggled in *one* chicken to place under Adelaide's bed. 'Tis a record, I think."

"And the little ones?"

"Hale and hearty," Mary said. "Emma will be crawling any day now."

"God help us," he muttered. But he had to admit, there was something so *hopeful* in watching a babe learn her way in the world. "The lessons have been going well?"

"Oh, aye!" As Mary launched into a description of her teachings, Merrick was content to just watch. He remembered her birth, when Anna had handed him the screaming infant. He'd been so unsure, and even his own father had urged him to set his bastard aside, as he himself had done many times. But when Mary had quieted and stared up at Merrick, he'd *known*. He'd known this child was his blood, his future.

The last seventeen years had passed in a blink, but had also seemed to drag on. How was it possible she was already a woman grown? A lass with a talent for keeping the bairns in line, a talent for teaching them what they needed to know. She'd be married soon enough, and making him a grandfather, although the thought soured his mood.

Irritated once more, he scrubbed his hands over his face and down his neck. Mary was seventeen. When had he gotten so *old*?

"Where's Andrew?" he asked gruffly.

"He's patrolling. He said that was what ye'd want him to do, to ensure our safety. I'll fetch him." She turned toward the door, then whirled back suddenly. "Oh! I forgot! He caught a *spy*!"

His senses sharpened, and Merrick took a step toward her. "Explain," he snapped.

She bobbed her head eagerly. "Andrew was patrolling and caught a Lowlander! He's in the dungeon right now!"

Merrick's hands tightened to fists by his side. "*Gavin!*" he roared. His second must've been standing out on the landing, because the man was at Mary's side in moments. "Fetch Andrew," Merrick commanded. "I want his report immediately."

Gavin slammed his fist into his chest and bowed before leaving. Mary hurried after him, probably intent on searching for her beau as well. Even the thought of his wee daughter interested in Andrew couldn't detract from Merrick's coiled anticipation.

He was torn between stalking to the dungeons himself and hearing the lad's report. He'd give Andrew a short time to appear, before taking the task himself. In the meantime, Merrick accepted the bread, cheese, and ale a servant offered.

He hadn't even finished the first flagon when Gavin returned, Andrew in tow. The lad was eager to tell of his success, and Merrick was impressed with his actions.

"Ye're sure this spy is a Lindsay?"

Andrew nodded. "He's dressed in Lowlander fashion, milord, and was on yer land, headed for the keep. Who else would he be?"

It was hard to deny. Merrick was ready to meet this spy. "Gavin?"

His second nodded and hurried for the kitchens, obviously intent on making up for his failure to track Lindsay's men. He must've gathered men to search for Andrew, because more and more Sutherland warriors had trickled in during the lad's story, as well as servants and workers. Now, Merrick listened to their murmurs and whispers as they waited for the spy to be brought in.

And he shared their anticipation. *A Lindsay!* If Merrick really held a Lindsay, one of his bastard brother's men, here in the keep, he held *power*. Not just to negotiate, but to learn what Lindsay's plans were beyond "make life miserable for the Sutherlands and their laird."

He felt himself grinning, and didn't bother to hide it.

Gavin returned quickly, and Merrick almost thought him alone. But his second stepped through the stone doorway and pulled a figure behind him, and Merrick realized why he hadn't seen the spy.

It was a lad. A lad younger than Andrew, younger even than Willie.

Merrick swallowed down a spike of anger at his brother for using a lad this young. John Lindsay had proven he wasn't above such tactics, and Merrick couldn't afford to let pity blind him. Instead, he studied the shrunken figure dispassionately.

Gavin hadn't bothered to do aught more than tying the lad's hands, and it was clear why. Hunched as he was, small as he was, he offered no danger to the looming wall of Highlanders surrounding him.

Andrew had been right; the lad was clearly dressed in Lowlander fashion. His breeches were torn, and the linen on his sleeves was filthy—from the dungeon or before? Although he wore no colors, it was likely he was a Lindsay, or at least allied with them.

"What's yer name?" Merrick barked.

When the lad didn't answer, Gavin gave him a shake by the upper arm, then pushed him forward. He stumbled closer to Merrick, and stood with his head bowed and his tied arms hanging limp before him.

Merrick didn't like being ignored. "I willnae ask again," he growled.

Finally, the lad lifted his head to stare dazedly at Merrick, who wondered if maybe he'd suffered a head injury to explain the confusion in his gaze. The lad looked half-dead with his gaunt cheeks and that light hair hanging lank around his face.

Merrick spoke to Andrew without dropping his glare from the spy. "When was the last time he was fed?"

From the corner of his eye, he saw his former squire shrug. "We captured him the day after ye left."

Three days the lad had been in the dungeons. Three days

without food? Had he been given water? If not, that might explain why the lad was now eying the flagon of ale on the table behind Merrick.

He might have the reputation of a Devil, but he'd learned long ago that justice should be a swift mercy. Torturing this spy would serve him poorly.

So he did as he said he would not. "Lad?" he prompted again, trying to gentle his voice. "What is yer name?"

The boy dragged his attention back to Merrick. God's wounds, but he looked weak. His legs were wobbling, he was leaning too far forward, and his eyes were cloudy. Was the lad ill?

Merrick took a step closer, intent only on catching him if he fell over, but the lad jerked as if he'd been struck. His tongue dragged out across his cracked lips.

"S— Saf," the lad croaked in a ragged whisper.

Nodding, hoping to encourage the boy, Merrick stepped closer again. "And what are ye doing on Sutherland land, Saf?"

"I…" The spy shook his head, a little too hard, as if trying to regain his wits. "Nay," he croaked. He managed to pale even further, and looked in danger of collapsing. His confusion didn't appear feigned.

Either he was a brilliant actor, or he was genuinely close to fainting.

"Saf," Merrick barked again, hoping to gain the lad's attention.

The spy's gaze jerked to his, and Merrick was surprised to see they were a brilliant blue under the haze of hunger and confusion and desperation. He began to reach for the lad.

"Aye, milord?" came the ragged whisper, right before the lad folded over.

Merrick was there before he made it halfway down, scooping the lad into his arms, and pulling him against his chest.

He froze.

Lad? Nay.

Merrick cradled the still figure, and the chest binding was unmistakable. He patted the back of the surcoat, just to be sure. Aye, those were bindings, worn under the shirt.

And pressed against his chest? Those were definitely breasts.

This lad—Saf?—was a *lass.*

He stared down at her face, visible now that her head had lolled back. Under the dirt she might be pretty. It was hard to tell. How old was she? Older than Willie, surely. Older than Mary?

What was she doing spying for a bastard like Lindsay?

And why should he keep her secret?

From behind him, Gavin cleared his throat. "Laird?"

He focused on the present situation. "This lad kens naught of violence, 'tis obvious." He'd decided to hide her sex. She must have a reason, and he had power over her if she didn't think he knew her secret. She'd be more likely to reveal her reason for being here if she felt safe. Assuming she lived.

"He needs food and water. He'll tell us more if he feels safe."

It was impossible to miss the way Andrew scoffed. "He'll tell ye everything ye wish to know, Laird."

"Aye, once he's been fed." Shifting her in his arms, he called out to one of the servants, "Have Corra send supper to my room. I'll eat there and make sure the lad does as well."

"Is that safe, milord?"

Merrick whirled on his former squire. "Ye'd question me?" he roared, disturbed to notice the lass in his arms didn't even flinch at the sound. He took a breath, willing himself to adopt an instructive tone. "Have I no' always told ye 'tis easier to win enemies with offers of peace?"

Andrew's response was swift. "Nay, Laird."

Hmm. "What have I taught ye, then?"

Again, the reply was immediate, "To act swiftly."

"Aye," Merrick agreed. "Because justice served swiftly is a mercy."

He'd learned that lesson over a decade ago. He'd been riding with Duncan Sinclair, and they'd caught another lad guilty of sheep-thieving. Merrick hadn't been able to punish the rest of the band, but he'd strung the lad up.

But he hadn't died quickly, and the longer he watched the lad—only a bit older than Willie was now—struggle, the more uncomfortable he'd become. He hadn't objected when, with a curse, Duncan Sinclair had cut the boy down. The former sheep thief had found a place at Duncan's side as a bodyguard.

Although the thief had grown into a loyal guard, he'd deserved the punishment Merrick had meted out all those years ago. And if Merrick had acted more swiftly, the Sinclair Hound would be dead now…but he wouldn't have suffered.

He shook himself, aware his men were watching. "A good leader kens when to take his time as well, lad," he said gruffly. "This spy will tell us naught if he dies."

Gavin was nodding in support. "And he's clearly no threat. Mayhap his loyalty could be bought."

"Aye." Merrick grunted as he lifted the lass over his shoulder, so she hung down like a sack. He sent a small grin toward Andrew. "Besides, I have need of a new squire."

Andrew's roar of disapproval followed Merrick up the steps to the laird's chamber, and his grin grew. The lad had to learn when to question his laird, and when to keep his mouth shut. Threatening to give this Lindsay spy his highly-coveted position of squire was more than enough to irritate Andrew.

Corra had anticipated his request; supper was already waiting for him as he pushed open the door to his chamber. And as much as he wanted that stew and ale, the lass needed it more. Nay, she needed water first.

Gently, Merrick pulled the lass from his shoulder and tried to stand her upright, her head lolling against his chest. He reached for the ewer of water which always stood beside a basin on his father's trunk. He cradled her in the crook of his arm and nudged her head forward. When she was positioned correctly, he used his other hand to dripple water past her lips.

He found himself whispering a silent prayer for her survival.

For the information she can give me, naught else.

He almost believed himself.

He watched her swallow, then swallow again as he offered her more water. Finally, she started to breathe a little easier. Still, it was another age before she began to revive… her eyes opened and she snatched the ewer from his hands.

"Easy, Saf," he murmured as she guzzled the water. "Easy, la —lad." He reminded himself of his earlier decision. If she didn't know he was aware of her secret, she'd be more open with him. "Too much will—aye, that."

He held the basin while she vomited, then set her in a chair and poured her a smaller glass.

"Slower," he commanded, and saints be praised, she followed his commands.

The act of drinking seemed to exhaust her, but it was more likely the culmination of her last days. She swallowed the last mouthful and rested her head against the wooden back of the chair with a soft exhalation.

"Eat, Saf," he urged gently.

When she ignored his offering of bread, he frowned, worried she was in worse shape than he'd thought. He dipped the brown bread in the ale, then held it against her lips. To his relief, they parted, and after a long moment, she swallowed the soft food.

It was a slow process, but he continued to feed her, though the task was below a laird. She finished more bread and drank more water, but her eyes remained unfocused and closed most of the time. When they did open, she seemed not to understand where she was or what was happening.

Who is she?

The question was impossible to answer, not with her in this state. Eventually, there was a moment when she would eat no more, and Merrick realized she'd passed out again. Asleep or another faint? Or was there something more treacherous afoot here?

When she began to tip forward, he caught her once more, and lifted her in his arms the way he might Adelaide or little hellion Eva. Saf was older, definitely, but felt just as small. He took the time to study her.

She had high cheekbones and pale skin, although that might've been because of her imprisonment. And aye, her hair was a rat's nest and she was filthy. He lifted one of her hands, turning it over to examine the broken nails. Again, evidence of a hard adventure, but her fingers weren't callused. Only a rough spot between her thumb and forefinger, where one might hold a stylus, seemed permanent. The blisters and bruises were more recent.

Hmm.

He placed her on his large bed, then stood staring down at her.

She was no servant or crofter, and not used to hard labor. It was impossible to imagine a *lady* in her current position, but her hands didn't lie. If she was a Lindsay, was she one of the laird's family? John's cousin or sister?

Or—Merrick's hands fisted at the thought—his whore?

Mayhap she was no lady at all, but another position used to ease. But why would she be spying for Lindsay dressed as a lad?

There was no way of knowing until she recovered enough to tell him. Although it was hard to believe she'd wake before tomorrow, Merrick secured the weapons in the room before moving the food to the table beside the bed. He'd leave her in his room tonight and sleep elsewhere.

She'd eventually tell him what he needed to know.

He vowed it.

CHAPTER 4

FROM THE TIME she was a young girl, Saffy had woken easily. She'd shared a bed with various sisters over the years—sometimes all three!—and had gotten used to Citrine's early-morning jolting-upright-in-bed. Saffy would then wake, but would often hold herself still while Citrine thrashed about, attempting to extricate herself from the coverlet. *That's* how Saffy often got accused of having bony knees, although it was obviously not the case. It was just Citrine, flopping around.

The memories of Citrine jolting the bed were what had Saffy confused this morning. She was lying on a comfortable mattress, aye, but she was perfectly still. Her twin wasn't making her bounce about. Now that Pearl and Agata were married, Citrine would be the only one sharing a mattress with Saffy, and she was unnaturally still. Had she awakened already?

For that matter, it was obviously well past dawn; the sunlight streaming in through the open window attested to that. Why had she slept so late? And where were the familiar tapestries she'd come to know over the years? The room looked completely different. These tapestries were done in reds and blacks instead of blues and greens, and showed battle scenes, like a warrior might prefer. And the goblets on the far table weren't something she or her sisters might use.

She blinked slowly, trying to make sense of what she was seeing.

This wasn't her room, was it?

Nay, she'd been…she'd left home, hadn't she? Traveling to Dornach with Munro, then further alone. Dressed as a lad. Sleeping on the ground.

Exhaustion.

Being captured by the Sutherland and accused of spying!

The dungeon!

The hunger, the weakness, the hopelessness!

The memories slammed into her, and Saffy pushed herself upright in the bed, the coverlet falling across her lap.

She touched her hair, and wasn't sure if she was relieved or horrified to know she hadn't imagined being dressed as a lad. Despite the sumptuous bed, she was still wearing the surcoat and braies, and when she wiggled her toes, she could feel the stockings. Her hands were filthy, and she imagined the rest of her was as well.

The days and nights in the Sutherland dungeon had taken their toll on her.

Her stomach rumbled, reminding her of hunger, but surprisingly, it wasn't as strong as she remembered. And there was a stale taste on her tongue—ale?

There was…there'd been a man. She remembered being scared, but he'd held her gently and… She closed her eyes, the effort of remembering making her head hurt. He'd fed her, hadn't he? He'd worn Sutherland colors, and she'd been terrified, but he'd fed her and spoken soothingly, as if she'd been a bairn.

"Ye're awake, then?"

The voice—a low rumble—came from across the room,

and Saffy's eyes flew open. When she saw the strange man slouched in the chair, flipping the short dirk back and forth, she sucked in a breath. He was wearing Sutherland colors! Heart racing, she scrambled back against the headboard, as if the bed covers would offer her some protection.

But instead of pouncing, the man *chuckled* as he pushed himself upright.

And Saffy sucked in another breath for an entirely different reason.

Dear God, the man was *beautiful*.

His dark hair had flashes of silver at the temples and was cropped close. The color matched the short stubble on his cheeks, as if he hadn't yet scraped his chin that day, as many warriors preferred. And his eyes…his eyes were striking. A blue so pale it looked like ice, but surrounded by a dark ring so that he looked at the world through a tunnel.

Her own eyes widened at the sight, mesmerized by his features.

And then his lips twitched, and his amused gaze was so intriguing, she swore she stopped breathing.

Her sisters had mentioned this, this *wanting* when a beautiful man smiled. Agata and Citrine had talked about the way a man could make heat pool deep in their bellies, to make a woman want to squirm. And Saffy had seen attractive men before, of course, but *this* one…

Mayhap it was his age. He looked like a man experienced enough to know what a woman wanted. Mayhap it was his eyes, or his smile, or those high cheekbones.

All she knew was that she was sitting in a strange bed, dressed as a lad, and on a mission to save her family…and she very much wanted to touch this man.

Sutherland or not, she wanted to *kiss* him. And that was something she absolutely could *not* do, not if she wanted her mission to be successful.

Slowly, he stood. Her eyes went wider as she took in all of him, from his simple linen shirt to the plaid slung low on his hips, to the way he slipped the long dirk into the sheath on his belt, to his strong legs and boots.

Her gaze lingered on his hands, and she had the strangest feeling they'd touched her before.

"Aye, Saf," he said with a rumble. "I was the one who fed ye yesterday."

Yesterday? She glanced at the window. It was late afternoon already. She'd been asleep for more than a day? Her stomach growled again, and he jerked his chin in reaction.

"There's more food for ye."

He crossed to a table and picked up a tray, which he carried to the bed. "Can ye feed yerself? Or do I need—"

"I can do it," she hurried to reassure him, alarmed at how rough her voice sounded.

As much as Saffy wanted the man to sit beside her and treat her gently, *Saf the lad* wouldn't want that. Boys were independent, and would hate to have him fussing over her.

Him.

Whatever.

She scowled at her own thoughts and reached for the bread. After dipping it in the ale, she took a small bite, and the flavor brought back a memory. Her gaze flashed to him.

He *had* fed her, hadn't he? She remembered him carefully pushing a piece of ale-soaked bread between her lips. He'd treated her so gently, and he knew her name.

The man was stretching, as if his muscles were kinked. She chewed slowly and watched him, trying to keep the interest out of her gaze, afraid she was revealing too much of her feelings. When he finished, he crossed his arms and propped his hip against the windowsill. Lit from behind by the late afternoon sun, he looked like some kind of…

Saffy shook her head. She definitely did *not* believe in the fairies and little people, but couldn't deny he looked other-worldly. Angelic? Nay, harder than that.

The longer he watched her eat, the more his silent stares began to unnerve her.

"Thank ye," she managed to croak. "I was…I needed…"

"Food, aye. And water." He gave a curt nod. "I've come in several times since last night to make sure ye drank water, but I didnae think ye'd remember."

He'd given her water, even if she was asleep? That would explain the way her now-full stomach was pushing against her bladder. Still, she could do naught about it until he left, so she reached for the hunk of cheese and bit into it, trying to distract her mind.

She could swear he'd narrowed his eyes. "'Twas the least I could do," he said entirely too nonchalantly, "after Andrew locked ye in my dungeon."

My dungeon.

Saffy froze, the bite of cheese turning sour on her tongue.

My dungeon.

He was… Her heart began to pound again. He was a Sutherland, and called the dungeons *his*? Did that mean the keep was his, too? If so, he was… He was…

Oh, dear God.

His brow twitched. "I've surprised ye? Allow me to intro-duce myself." He stepped away from the window and bowed briefly. "Merrick Sutherland, laird of this clan."

The Sutherland Devil.

Saffy began to choke on the now-dry cheese in her mouth, and reached for the flagon of ale to wash it down. Forcing herself to concentrate on not choking to death, she closed her eyes and tried not to think of what this meant.

She was in the same room as the most ruthless laird in the Highlands! A man she'd heard horror stories about! A man she absolutely *did not* want to be at the mercy of.

A man who held ye gently and made sure ye were fed and watered.

The Sutherland Devil!

He does no' look like a devil.

She forced steady breaths as she lowered the flagon.

Nay, he didn't look like a devil, did he? With those fascinating eyes and that otherworldly glow.

The Devil is otherworldly, is he no'?

Whose side was her mind on, anyhow?

He was watching her reaction—and her internal argument, likely. He looked amused.

"Ye were not expecting a laird to be watching ye sleep, waiting for ye to awake?"

It was as good an excuse as any. "Aye," she croaked. "That's it." She began to tear the bread into small pieces, hoping to hide her shaking hands.

He shrugged and propped his hip against the window ledge once more. "Get used to it," he said. "Ye're in my keep, and I intend to learn everything I can about ye, *Saf.*"

"Why?" she'd blurted before she could think better of it.

"Because I want to ken what Lindsay is up to, and I think ye can tell me."

Lindsay? The lad who'd captured her—Andrew—had used that name, too. He'd called her a spy for Lindsay, but she didn't know what he'd meant.

Shaking her head, she tried to arrange her words. "I...I'm no' a spy. Andrew called me that, but I'm no'. Truly."

His brow twitched. "That's what a spy would say."

"Aye, and also what an innocent...lad would say." She hoped he hadn't noticed the slight hesitation and pushed on before he could, hoping to put him on the defensive. "I came to yer home, looking for work."

"Dressed as a Lowlander?" he shot back.

Surprised, she glanced down at her clothing. "'Tis no' such unusual dress. Men of my clan wear this in the winter."

"And what clan is that?"

When she saw the hungry look in his eyes, she winced, knowing she'd given away too much. "I'd—I cannae say."

"Cannae or willnae?"

He was no dullard, that was for certain. Saffy felt her palms begin to sweat, and unconsciously, swiped them down the woolen blanket.

"I…I only wanted someplace to stay. A job."

He nodded briskly. "Aye, and ye'll have one, here where I can learn yer secrets, Saf. Where are ye from?"

She shook her head, knowing she couldn't answer him. Things were getting hazy again. Dear God, this man—this gorgeous man—had been contracted to marry her sister Pearl! What would he do if he discovered her identity?

He wasn't discouraged, though. "Ye spent three days in my dungeon without food or water. I was the one who dragged ye out of there and saved yer life. Ye owe me."

"Nay," she whispered, alarmed at how hard it was to think. She was still so very tired.

"Aye, and now I own *ye*."

Own…

He's the Devil, remember?

She shook her head.

Suddenly, he loomed over her, pulling the tray from the bed and depositing it on the nearby table. She stared up at him mutely.

"What did ye do during those three days, Saf?" he asked softer.

Do?

"To keep yer mind sharp, lad. What did ye do to keep from going mad?"

It was a simple enough question, and at that moment, she

couldn't think of a lie to tell him. Couldn't think of a reason to lie to him. "I corrected the graffiti," she said simply.

His teeth flashed as he grinned lightning-quick, his serious expression settling once more onto his full lips. "As I recall, my grandfather imprisoned his brother-in-law for a while down there, waiting for permission to marry his sister. My great uncle kenned quite the collection of curses."

Thinking of the things carved into the stone far below, Saf nodded silently.

Quick as a flash, the Sutherland darted forward and lifted her right hand from where it rested on the coverlet. "A knowledge of Latin would also explain this," he said as he flipped her hand over, his fingertips brushing against the callus on the outside of her forefinger.

And for the first time ever, her mind was struck completely and utterly blank.

Warmth from his touch spread up her hand and arm, filling her chest and making her gape at him. Dear God in Heaven, but his touch felt *divine*.

Devil, he may be, but he made her shiver like a saint.

And from the way his smile flashed again, just briefly, he knew it.

Ye're a lad!

Her mind finally started working again, and she yanked her hand from his with a gasp. She was supposed to be *Saf*, a lad looking for work. If she sat here and mooned over this gorgeous devil, shivering at his touch, and longing for more, her masquerade would be uncovered in a moment.

Trying to sound like one of her father's younger warriors, she made her voice gruff. "I have to…" She shook her head and shifted in the bed. "I need privacy."

Scooting to the other side of the bed, she swung her legs off, and braced herself against the wave of lightheadedness.

She was still so weak, so tired. At least her thirst had been quenched, but that meant…

When she pushed herself upright, leaning on the bedpost for support, she was surprised to still see the Devil across the room, staring at her with a glint of amusement in his eyes.

Oh. A lad wouldnae demand privacy, would he?

But she could no more relieve herself in front of him than she could reveal her identity. The two things were connected, in fact.

As much as she hated to push the fact, nature couldn't be denied. "Milord?"

Blandly, he raised one brow in challenge. "Aye, lad?"

"I need privacy," she stated again, feeling like a clot-heid.

He jerked his chin toward a screen in the corner. "By all means."

"Ye…ye plan to stay?"

"This is *my* chamber, Saf. Ye cannae kick me out."

Oh, God.

The journey to the other side of the room saw her stumbling once or twice, but he didn't move to help her, thank the saints. By the time she fumbled her way out of her braies and squatted over the pot, she was sure her cheeks were apple-red.

And then he began to whistle to cover the echoing sound of water hitting clay, and she closed her eyes in mortification.

Still, she managed to right herself and stumble from behind the screen once more. He stood in the same spot, looking far too comfortable. She eyed the bed, her entire body feeling *longing* to lie down once more. But instead, she thrust her chin out.

She couldn't look at him directly. "Now what?"

"Milord," he supplied helpfully.

Confused, her gaze darted to his, then down once more. "What?"

"Ye will call me milord. Or laird. Or Laird Sutherland."

Her nod of acknowledgement was more of a jerk, but she couldn't deny his censure. He might be the devil, but he *was* a laird. "My laird," she repeated softly, still staring at the brooch which held his plaid in place.

A brooch much like the missing Sinclair jewels.

"I like that," he said softly, then immediately cleared his throat. "Now what?" he prompted, reminding her of her earlier question.

She shrugged. "I wondered what other humiliations ye had planned for me."

And God love him, but he chuckled. It was over in a moment, but she was so surprised, she met his eyes once more.

"*Plenty*, wee Saf. I'm the Sutherland Devil, have ye no' heard?"

Entranced by the combination of humor and hardness in his eyes, Saffy felt herself nod.

"Despite my reputation, I dinnae believe in torture. But that willnae stop me from pressing ye, because I *will* learn yer secrets, Saf."

He pushed away from the window and began to stalk toward her. Saffy swallowed, knowing she had nowhere to run, and couldn't manage it, even if there *was* some place safe.

And a tiny part of her mind was yelling *Ye're safe with him!*

Stupid thought.

"I—I have nae secrets," she managed to choke out.

He halted right in front of her, close enough to touch. It felt as if he *was* touching her, the way she was completely aware of his body, his warmth. She held her breath as she tilted her head back and forced herself to meet his eyes.

"I think ye do, Saf," he whispered, his stare intense. "And I'll learn them."

Her mouth worked, but she could think of no denial. Finally, she shook her head slightly.

And he nodded in return.

"Ye're mine now, wee Saf. Ye wanted a job? I have one for ye, a coveted position."

The way he was looking at her...Saffy swallowed and reminded herself he thought she was a *lad*.

"Aye?" she croaked.

"Aye, *milord*," he prompted her.

Arrogant man. "Aye...*Devil?*"

He grinned again, and while one part of her was relieved he hadn't punished her for sass, another part wished his smile didn't make him look quite so...approachable.

'Tis hard to call him a devil when he smiles like that.

"I'm going to make ye my squire." Before she could process what that meant, he placed one palm against the wall by her head and leaned forward. "Ye'll tend to my needs, ye'll attend me in practice and at meals, and ye'll devote yer every waking moment to *me*."

Dear God in Heaven.

Saffy was sure the exhaustion was overtaking her. *Surely* that explained why her limbs felt so weak, why her heart was pounding so fast, as she stared at the lips which had just uttered those impossible words.

Stay with him? Attend him? She managed a little head shake.

Those arrogant, devilish lips curved upward just slightly. "Oh, aye, wee Saf," he growled. "And ye'll sleep here in this chamber. With me."

Saffy's knees gave out.

And before she could hit the ground, he was there, scooping her up. Before she could blink, she was cradled in his arms, tucked safely against his chest.

It was the oddest sort of horror and anticipation, wrapped up in warmth. Did he intend for her to share his bed *now*? As intrigued as she was by the possibility, she couldn't afford to assuage her curiosity about the *Sutherland Devil*.

Besides, he thinks ye a lad.

She began to kick. "Put me down," she demanded, as fiercely as she could manage, trying to twist out of his grip.

He merely held her tighter and chuckled. She stilled when she felt his laughter where her shoulder was pressed against his chest.

And then he was placing her on the bed once more, pulling the cover up around her. "I'll give ye one more night here alone, Saf. Starting tomorrow, I'm taking my bed back, and ye can have the pallet." He stepped back and stared down at her thoughtfully. "And I willnae be here when ye wake, ye have my word. There's always water in that ewer"—he jerked his chin toward the far table—"if ye need to wash. And since ye'll be attending me, ye *will* wash."

Laying as stiff as a corpse, Saffy could do no more than gape at him. He hadn't meant for her to share the bed with him? He was allowing her more rest? He wanted her to be *clean?*

Relief shot through her so fast, she thought she might faint again. "Aye," she whispered.

He looked as if he might say more, but then snapped his mouth shut and spun toward the door. She heard him bellowing orders as soon as he was in the hall, and didn't miss the sound of something heavy being pushed in front of the door.

To prevent her escape?

She stared at the ceiling and exhaled heavily. She had no *need* to escape. While meeting the Sutherland laird had been the very last thing she'd wanted to do—*ever*—she'd done it and was still alive. *And* he'd given her an excuse to stay here in the keep! Being by his side all the time meant she wouldn't have time to search for her family's jewels, but surely, she'd be able to sneak away a bit? And being with him meant she'd hear everything he heard. She might be able to glean information which would help in her search.

Her eyelids felt heavy. Escape? She smirked as she rolled over on the comfortable pillows. She was well-fed and exhausted, and looking forward to the chance to be clean again. There was no way she'd try to escape.

Merrick Sutherland thought she was a lad. It was odd to think of the Sutherland Devil having a first name, but if she really was going to attend to him, she'd have to stop calling him *devil*. While he'd laughed the first time, he might not the next. From the stories she'd heard, he'd respond with a swift blow, especially since he believed her a lad.

And he'd called her *Saf*, so her secret was still safe.

I will learn yer secrets.

When he'd said that, it had sounded more like a promise than a threat.

She closed her eyes, her mind too numb to work through the logical outcomes of this situation. *Tomorrow.* Tomorrow she'd be rested and fed and clean and *then* she could figure out how she would find the next clue to the jewels' whereabouts.

Merrick.

He's called her *his*, which should've terrified her. But as sleep claimed her, Saffy knew one thing: she'd felt *safe* in his arms.

CHAPTER 5

SHE HEALED WELL. After that first encounter in his chamber, watching her sleeping so peacefully in his bed, Merrick had kept his distance. Not because he was being kind—he'd told her she'd be attending him every moment, after all—but because of his reaction to her.

She was filthy. She was dressed as a lad. He had no idea what she looked like under those ridiculous clothes.

But when he'd touched her, it'd felt…*right*.

Holding her, even just holding her hand, had made his skin itch and his muscles tense. A tightness deep in his belly reminded him of the long-ago way Anna had made me him feel.

He'd been so young then, barely twenty-two when he'd planted Mary in her belly. And Anna had been a vivacious and lusty wench, who met his passions head-on. It'd been no wonder he'd fallen hard for her, no wonder he still remembered those feelings.

But Saf—or whatever her name was—couldn't be more different than Anna. She was skinny where Anna had curves, pale where his leman had been dark…

And she had the most incredible eyes. Large and bright blue, the color of sapphires. They'd flashed open that afternoon in his chamber, and he'd been afraid he'd fall into them.

She'd met his warnings with sass, and in an effort to intimidate her, he'd gotten too close.

When he'd threatened to have her sleep with him, he saw the understanding in her eyes. She'd thought he'd meant to bed her, and God help him, but that's exactly what he'd meant. Of course, it'd been easy to claim he wanted her only to sleep on a pallet beside him, and he hadn't missed the flash of *something* in her expression then. Relief? Disappointment?

All he knew was that placing her back in that bed—alone—had required remarkable willpower.

She's a lad. Remember that.

He'd gone out to the training fields and beat Gavin, which made him feel a bit better. Of course, the next day, Gavin gave as good as he'd gotten, and they were both sporting new bruises.

Which was good, because lying there in his dark chamber that night, listening to her breathe softly on her pallet beside the bed, Merrick was glad for *any* distraction.

Four days after his return from his futile chase of his half-brother, Saf finally was well enough to venture from his chamber. She still wore that surcoat and breeches, but everything—including her—had been washed. Someone had given her a thong to tie her hair back, and freshly scrubbed, she looked much healthier.

That first evening at dinner in the great hall, he sat back in his chair and watched her bustle around the high table, rushing from one flagon to the next to refill ale, and he had to admit he was impressed. When she wasn't needed, she stepped down from the dais and just *observed.*

Those blue eyes flicked over all the children, lingering, flashing back and forth between him and Beck, who was one of the bairns who looked nothing like Merrick. He imagined he could hear her brain working.

What kind of woman corrected graffiti in a dungeon?

Unbidden, a smile flashed across his lips, and when she saw it, she flushed and looked away.

"Ye're in a good mood tonight, milord."

For the loyalty he'd shown in protecting the keep and Merrick's family, Andrew had been granted the honor of sitting at the high table once more. Merrick had been certain to place him opposite Mary this time—*And why the hell do I have to think about this kind of thing?*—but his former squire seemed eager to please.

Merrick lifted his flagon in acknowledgment. "Just thinking about tomorrow's training."

The young man nodded. "I'm looking forward to sparring with ye. And in a few days, ye'll be joining me to teach the lads, aye?"

Andrew was one of the youngest Sutherland warriors, although skilled. Attending Merrick for all the years he had, the young man had proven to be a fast learner, and now could hold his own against many of the older men. But Merrick had also put him in charge of training the lads who were not yet warriors, and was eager to see how they'd progressed.

He nodded and eyed Andrew's empty flagon. "Aye. And ye have need of more ale. *Saf!*" he bellowed.

When she came hurrying over, the pitcher in her hands, she was glaring at him. "Ye dinnae have to shout. I was right there."

Andrew gasped in shock at her cheekiness, and Merrick bit down on his smile. Not only could he not afford *her* to think he was easy to charm, he didn't want his men to know how amusing he found her.

He kept his voice mild when he reminded her, "*Milord.*"

She scowled as she topped off Andrew's flagon. "Aye,

milord. Anything else, *milord*?" Taking a small step back, she gave a flourishing curtsey.

Mayhap it was an accident. Mayhap it was part of her sarcasm. Had she bowed, it would've been obvious, but a lad curtseying had more than a few men erupting in laughter—Gavin the loudest.

Merrick had to lift his own flagon and take a long draught to hide his smile.

After she'd stepped back, Andrew seemed to regain his voice. "Laird! Allow me to train him. I'll beat some respect into that thick skull of his! He cannae speak to ye—"

"Aye, in good time," Merrick said with a casual wave. "We'll start the day after tomorrow. In the meantime, I'm learning plenty about our little interloper."

His former squire's eyes flashed, and he leaned forward. Gavin did the same, but he didn't look convinced.

"Have ye learned Lindsay's plans?" Andrew asked. "Has he told ye where the bastard will strike next?"

Merrick shook his head. Nay, no matter how many times he'd asked Saf—no matter which combination of questions or how off-guard he caught her—she still denied knowing anything about John Lindsay.

But he was learning all sorts of *other* things about her.

Like the fact she muttered in her sleep, women's names and talking about jewels. The fact her eyes flashed when she was irritated with him. The fact she not only could read, but enjoyed the trade agreements and treatises strewn over the desk in his solar. The fact she liked things tidy, and he often returned to his chamber and solar to find everything arranged much neater than Andrew had ever kept it.

Aye, he was learning plenty about *her*, but nothing about what he needed to know.

Andrew sat back with a scowl. "We need some way to

break him," he said, slamming his fist into his opposite palm. "He *must* tell us what he kens! Lindsay cannae—"

"I said I'll take care of Saf," Merrick growled in warning, "and I meant it. Ye'll leave him to me."

Andrew reluctantly nodded, and when Merrick glanced at Gavin, his second was staring at Saf with a thoughtful frown.

Merrick stifled his sigh, and cast about for some change in topic. He wasn't sure why, but the thought of either of these two—or any of his men—paying special attention to Saf...it irritated him.

"Is Elana enjoying her time with yer cousins?"

As soon as he'd blurted the question, Merrick regretted the distraction.

I'm pondering seating arrangements and his sister's social life?

What in damnation was going on with his mind?

And Gavin seemed equally uncomfortable about the topic. "She's fine," he said, reaching for his ale. "I assume. I...havenae heard much from her."

He didn't want to speak of his sister, and that was fine by Merrick. It had been a poor attempt at diversion anyhow. He nodded and turned to whatever Andrew was saying to the warrior on his right, and vowed to pay attention to clan matters.

Not matters pertaining to a certain intriguing young squire of his...

The next morning, she followed him to the training grounds. Per his instructions, Saf woke each morning before him and performed her own ablutions, then was ready to assist him. Of course, he needed no help, but he'd started to enjoy lying in his bed with his eyes cracked, watching her bustle around the room to put away her pallet and hurriedly wash herself.

It'd been hard not to laugh at her reaction the first time

she'd realized he slept nude. She'd all-but-tossed him his kilt, her cheeks a bright red.

They started their morning with her serving him porridge and following him on his duties. This morning it was training with his warriors.

She found a shaded spot and watched carefully. Although he needed to put her from his mind as he sparred, it was hard to ignore the fact she was staring at him. But rather than distract him, the knowledge she was watching made him work harder, pour more of his energy into the attacks and blocks, and even call out instructions as he saw fit.

Ye've still got life, auld man.

After, she trailed them all to the loch, but he noticed that as the warriors stripped and washed in the cold waters, she turned her shoulder and kept her attention firmly focused on the distant keep.

"He's no' one of Lindsay's men."

Gavin's casual pronouncement drew Merrick's attention. They were apart from the other men, up to their waists in the water.

"What makes ye say that?"

His second shrugged, frowning at Saf. "I cannae explain it. But...he watches everything ye do. Everything *we* do. I dinnae think he's used to being around so many men at one time."

Merrick straightened and nodded thoughtfully. "And ye think if he *were* one of Lindsay's men—a spy—he'd be more familiar with life in a band?"

"Aye. And he's nae crofter or servant, that much is obvious. So, who is he?"

Merrick grunted and scooped up another handful of water to slosh over his shoulder. "'Tis the question. I havenae decided yet, but I tend to agree with ye."

Until the words had left his mouth, Merrick hadn't realized that was his feeling. He didn't think Saf was one of his bastard brother's spies? Why not? Because he knew she was a female? Did he not think females capable of treachery?

Gavin had ducked under, and came up, shaking off his shaggy mane. "Ye havenae noticed him poking around the keep asking questions?"

"Nay, but he's only been well enough to be out of my chambers a few days."

"Keep an eye on him, Laird."

Merrick didn't need to be told twice.

He *did* keep an eye on Saf over the next few days, and not just because she was with him all the time. Andrew had never slept at the foot of his bed, like some sort of loyal hound. While Merrick had been the one to make the demand, wanting to ensure she wasn't sneaking off, he was coming to realize it meant she'd always be guarding her actions. It would've been smart to allow her more freedom and set a watcher on her.

But he'd grown used to having her in his room, in his life, and found himself making excuses to keep her close.

Aye, he watched her.

Watched her grow friendly with a few of his younger children. Watched her avoid Mary as much as possible—why? Was she afraid his oldest daughter would see through her disguise? He watched her charm his seneschal with her quick mind for numbers, and woo Corra into making Merrick's favorite venison dish again, after he'd mentioned his fondness for it.

She was taking her duties as his squire seriously, which was disconcerting.

If she'd been a lad, he would've guessed either she was a brilliant player, to appear so serious about her new position, *or* she was genuinely honored to become his squire.

But as a female, her reasons became much more tangled.

He was still mulling it over when she followed him to Andrew's training session a few days later. Andrew's lads, some of them still needed at home most days, had eagerly gathered to watch his demonstrations.

To their hungry stares, he spoke of how to counter strength and experience, and how to fight a much larger opponent. He taught them a few moves, then allowed a lucky few to practice on him.

"Should we give yer new squire a chance, laird?" Andrew called out.

Merrick could read his intent clearly. By giving Saf a sword and allowing her to attack, they might know if she really was a spy. But she was a lass! The thought made him frown, but he jerked his chin in agreement.

"Saf, to me."

She dragged her feet in attending him, and unlike other days, didn't wear a smirk. In fact, there was *worry* in her eyes.

He held out the small sword the lads used. "Have ye held one of these afore?"

"Aye," she said quietly, reaching for it.

To his surprise, she settled into the correct position, but didn't seem comfortable.

Without lifting his weapon, he beckoned her. "Ye were paying attention, aye? Show me what ye learned."

Her first attack was slow and clumsy, but she'd remembered his instructions, and hit him in the right places with the flat of her blade.

He exchanged glances with Andrew, who was looking begrudgingly impressed, then nodded once in approval. "Again," he commanded.

By her third try, she was flowing properly. He incorporated some of the other moves he'd taught the lads, and she met him blow for blow. She was weaker, obviously, and not nearly as comfortable with a blade as he was, but she'd obviously had some experience.

Interesting.

"Now, lad," he said, not even breathing heavily, "what would happen if I did *this?*"

On her next attack, he twisted out of the way. She followed, but was disconcerted by the shift. That little fact made it easy for him to thrust out a hip, knock her off balance, and trip her.

She rolled, of course, but he was tall enough it didn't matter. In two steps, he was able to go down to one knee beside her, his other booted foot planted by her shoulder, and his sword at her throat.

He'd done it for demonstration only. Not to get her at his mercy.

Oh, of course.

She should've been terrified. As far as she knew, he thought her a dangerous spy, and now she was lying beneath him, a blade to her throat. But her wide blue eyes were focused on his, and she seemed almost relaxed as she breathed carefully.

And her expression said she was merely curious what he'd do next.

Damn her and her inquisitive mind!

In an effort to unbalance her, he leaned forward until his mouth was close to her ear. "We could always grapple, next."

She blushed. An honest-to-God blush, but she didn't release his gaze as she quipped in return, "If that's what ye want, *Grandda.*"

Ah. There's the minx.

She was blushing at the thought of rolling around, learning the art of the grapple. *He* was in control here.

So why was he getting hard beneath his kilt?

"Two-score, *lad.*"

She blinked in confusion. "What?"

Pleased to have unbalanced her—*finally*—Merrick sheathed his sword and raised his voice so the other lads could hear. "I'm no' even two-score years." Winking lewdly, he did his best to lend credence to the rumors surrounding him, and discomfit her further, by continuing. "Aye, 'tis possible I'm a grandda, although I havenae heard the news. But wee Emma is but six months, so I can still make a lass moan in pleasure."

When Saf squeezed her eyes shut on a "Dear Lord," Merrick almost burst out laughing. It was satisfying to know he could meet her teasing head-on like that, and embarrass her in return.

Still, that's not why they were there.

He turned his attention to the other lads. "Ye see this position?" He was kneeling over Saf. "The enemy nae longer holds a sword to Saf's throat, aye? What could sh—*he* do to gain victory?"

Most of the pupils were silent, but one enthusiastic lad called out, "Knee ye in the bollocks, Laird!"

"Aye, good." He nodded, and spoke to Saf. "Yer limbs arenae tied. With the immediate threat removed, do what ye must to get free."

Eyes wide as she listened—he liked that she learned so quickly—she nodded slowly. "And..."

While he'd been distracted, she'd removed the dirk from her belt, and raised it to show him. He found himself smiling —him! Smiling during training!—at the adorable combination of fierceness and timidity.

"Good." He took her wrist to guide her hand, but spoke to all of his pupils. "In this case, there's nae need to even reveal yer hand. There's a vein here that will cause yer opponent to bleed out in minutes." He guided her hand—the dirk still gripped tightly in it—to his inner thigh, beneath his kilt.

He promised himself it was merely training, and he'd do the same for any of the other lads. But would they blush this way?

She wasn't breathing.

When she twitched away from his hold, he decided to take pity on her, and guided her hand to his hip. "A gut wound from a dagger willnae kill him quickly, but here"—he placed the dirk near his armpit—"will. And of course, the throat is the best option, if ye can reach it."

"Throat, armpit, bollocks." Her voice was a little hoarse. "Ye're certainly providing an education, Devil."

Pressing his lips together to hold back his snort, Merrick surged to his feet, and pulled her up with him. Her hand had been *under* his kilt, even if it had been for training, and even if she had been holding a dirk.

But his cock hadn't cared about that.

What would it feel like to have her hand under there again? Holding him, stroking him?

He muttered a curse and pushed himself away from her, determined to teach these lads something useful today.

And did his best to forget the feel of her skin under his fingers.

But that night, long after the training session was over, long after he'd bid his family goodnight and retired to his chambers, long after she'd curled up on her pallet and her breathing evened out, he found himself staring at the ceiling, thinking of her blush.

She'd kenned what I meant when I spoke of grappling. 'Twas why she'd called him "grandda".

Was it possible she felt this…this *whatever* it was? This tug between them? Merrick stacked one forearm behind his head and let out a breath.

Anna had been the last woman to arouse him this way. He was not like his father and uncles; despite his two failed marriages, Anna still held his heart.

Didn't she?

So many years had passed since her death, he'd gotten used to life without her. Without *any* woman. Elizabeth and

Katharine hadn't been real companions. These days, it was only Mary's smile and his empty bed which reminded him of the woman he'd once loved.

He hadn't felt that craving in a long while.

But since holding Saf in his arms...

She was cheeky and bright and had a sense of humor he liked. Had she been a lad, he would've made her his squire just to keep her around and lighten his mood.

But he couldn't forget the feel of those breasts under his touch, or the slenderness of her waist. What would she look like without that disguise? Would she be as pretty as he suspected? Would her body be as pale as the rest of her, all womanly curves? Would her breasts ache after being bound for so long, and be eager for his touch?

How would she taste?

With a groan, Merrick reached under the wool covers and grasped his already-thick cock. A few tugs, and he was as hard as he'd been earlier, kneeling above her.

He imagined her climbing on top of him in bed, of riding him with her hair falling wildly around her shoulders. He imagined her meeting him thrust for thrust.

And despite the fact she still called him *devil*, he imagined her *liking* being bedded by him.

He closed his eyes as he pumped, remembering the look in her eyes when he'd suggested she sleep with him, and knew desire when he'd seen it. He braced his heels, tenting the coverlet, and tried to control his breathing.

Apparently, he wasn't successful.

As his bollocks tightened, he knew he was moments from spilling against his belly, he heard her shift, then roll over.

"Milord?"

He froze, panting, wondering what noise he'd made.

"Laird Sutherland?" she asked again in that sleepy voice.

"Aye, Saf?" he managed to grind out.

A pause. Then, sleepily, "Do ye have need of me?"

Do ye have need of me?

Her question pounded a refrain in his mind.

Aye! Aye, in a hundred different ways!

Did she know what he was doing? What he was thinking about? Was she welcoming him to invite her to participate? Or did she mean it more innocently? Mayhap she thought he was thirsty or something?

As much as he wanted to command her to climb off her pallet and join him in this bed, as much as he wanted to tell her to *take care of him*, he knew he couldn't.

Bedding her was a complication he couldn't afford. He still wasn't convinced she wasn't a spy, and he wouldn't be able to think objectively if his attention was on her tits.

Besides, he didn't need any more bairns.

"Nay," he managed to choke out. "Go to sleep."

"Aye, Devil," she murmured.

He lay there, softening cock in hand, and listened to her breathing slowly even out once more. And he cursed himself.

It was a long night.

CHAPTER 6

ATTENDING the Sutherland Devil wasn't the worst thing in the world.

Saffy had been surprised by that realization. She'd expected to be treated like a servant, and was prepared to hate the man. But for every command he gave, every request he made, he also took the time to teach her something, as if she were a lad genuinely interested in learning to become a warrior.

And after the first few days, he began asking her opinion on things—particularly when they worked with his seneschal in the solar. *That* had made her more pleased than she'd expected.

Aye, she hadn't expected to *enjoy* being with him...but she was learning more things than she ever guessed about running a powerful clan, and to a woman whose mind was constantly whirling, it was a gratifying experience.

It was almost worth not having a moment to herself to look for the jewels!

Still, after more than a sennight had passed since her arrival, when he dismissed her for the morning while he went to train with his men, she didn't miss the opportunity to poke around the keep.

So far, her casual investigations hadn't been successful. Of course, she was befriending many Sutherlands, but it wasn't as if she could sidle up to them and say, "Have ye seen any evidence of hidden Sinclair jewels about?"

In fact, there wasn't anything she could say which wouldn't be suspicious. So, she knew she was on her own and used the opportunity to the best of her ability.

Whereas Citrine was a woman of action, Saffy was a scholar. It would make the most sense to read through the clan's histories, and she'd had that chance a few days ago in Merrick's solar. She'd learned his grandmother had, in fact, been a Campbell, but she'd known that already. There'd been no reference to jewels or the Sinclairs.

Now she was studying the tapestries. After all, the very first clue, which had sent Agata to the Mackenzies, had been hidden in an old tapestry, and many clans recorded important events in tapestries. She'd already examined all the ones hanging in the great hall and the laird's chambers, and now was working her way through the rest of the chambers.

Shouts and laughter wafted up from the courtyard, and Saffy stopped her futile search long enough to peer out the window at the end of the corridor. A smile came to her lips as she watched Merrick's children chasing one another below.

Merrick.

When had she begun to truly think of him that way? When had she begun to see him as a man?

Mayhap the first time she'd seen him lift wee Eva onto his lap as she angrily explained her younger brother's actions. Or the first time he'd patted stout Nolan on his shoulder. Or...

She shook her head and rested her forearms on the ledge, watching Beck chase Eva with something small and furry as Maggie fought an imaginary opponent. Adelaide sat in the sun, embroidering something, while their nurse played a game with little Isobel.

There were so many rumors surrounding the Sutherland Devil… That he acted swiftly, and without mercy. That he'd murdered his own brother, and from what she'd learned about his current troubles, he was at war with another brother. That his father had sired numerous bastards, as had he, none of whom the Sutherlands bothered claiming.

But…the last one clearly wasn't true. She was watching his brood now, and knew not only had he claimed them, but cared for them.

When he was with them, when they called him "Da", he was Merrick, *not* the Sutherland Devil.

A chuckle escaped Saffy's lips as Eva turned around and stuck out a foot, trying to trip Beck. He stumbled—catching himself at the last minute—and flung whatever he'd been holding at her. And Eva, bless her heart, *caught* the creature and carefully set it down, allowing it to scamper off.

Eva had her father's dark hair, but that was all they shared. Most of the other bairns must've taken after their mothers. Mary was the only one with her father's unusual eyes, although Saffy had heard the absent Willie took after his sire as well. The other children had light hair and brown eyes. Wee Beck looked angelic—until he smiled, and then it was clear he was planning something.

Shaking her head and still smiling, Saffy straightened. She needed to continue her search.

She was approaching the last chamber on this level—one she knew belonged to the children—when she heard murmurs. She stopped and cocked her head, hoping to determine who it was, but had no luck.

Well, they already think ye a spy, lass. Prove them right!

Smirking, she shook her head, knowing her inquisitive mind was going to get her in trouble.

Still, she cautiously stepped closer, hoping the clomp of her shoes wouldn't alert whomever was speaking. Mayhap it had, because the voices had stopped.

To be replaced by a damp, *squishy* noise.

What in the world?

Slowly, she poked her head around the edge of the open door and was surprised to see Mary in Andrew's arms.

Kissing him.

Ah. Well, that explains it.

The couple suddenly broke apart, Andrew shoving the lass behind him, his hand reaching for the dirk at his belt.

When Saffy stepped into the doorway, neither relaxed.

The three of them eyed each other warily, but Saffy's eyes were on Mary. Merrick's eldest daughter had struck her as intelligent and loyal, and had looked at "Saf" with far too much interest. At first, Saffy had thought the lass might've thought her a handsome lad, but once she realized Mary's heart belonged to Andrew, had become worried Merrick's daughter had seen through her disguise.

Saffy had avoided Mary since that realization, and wasn't comfortable with the calculating look in the girl's striking eyes now.

"What are ye doing here?" Andrew finally blurted.

He was clearly on the defensive and hadn't lowered his hand from his dirk. Saffy shrugged and told the truth.

"The laird gave me the morning away, and I'm interested in tapestries."

"Tapestries?" Andrew repeated skeptically.

Saffy jerked her chin toward the wall. "Those colorful wooly things. They insulate rooms, aye, but they're useful for—"

"I ken what tapestries are!" Andrew snapped. "*Why* are ye looking at them?"

"Because they tell stories," Saffy said slowly, as if the young warrior was hard of understanding. "And I like stories. Do *ye* like stories, Andrew?"

God's teeth, but it was hard not to laugh at the flash of fury in Andrew's face. Served him right for throwing her in a dungeon for three days!

Growling, Andrew stepped for her threateningly, but Mary pulled him back.

"Peace, love," she murmured soothingly. "Saf is just teasing ye."

He blinked and frowned. "He is *spying*. He's a spy, sent by Lindsay, and now he's poking around the keep, looking for information."

Saffy nodded solemnly. "Aye. Yer laird's enemy is *verra* interested in what his daughter is doing with his former squire."

While Andrew paled, Mary pressed her lips together. In disapproval? Or to hide a smile?

Saffy sighed. "I'm really just looking at the tapestries. I like history."

"Ye're no' spying on us?" he asked.

Part of her wanted to make him squirm, to pay him back in part for the misery he'd caused her, but it almost wasn't worth the effort.

"If I *were* spying on ye, I wouldnae be reporting to Lindsay. Do ye no' think Mary's father would be more interested in what I've seen?"

Andrew stiffened. "Laird Sutherland trusts me!" he declared, but there was a trace of doubt in his voice.

"Then ye have naught to worry about."

"Are ye going to tell him?" Andrew pressed.

Saffy met Mary's gaze over his shoulder. There was something in the lass's eyes…a *knowing*. It was hard to identify, but Saffy knew she wouldn't betray Mary's confidence. Not if there was a chance Mary could betray *hers*.

She shook her head. "Nay. Yer secret is safe."

Instead of looking relieved, an expression of confusion crossed Andrew's face.

As Saffy ducked out of the room and continued her search, she realized what it'd meant. The young warrior had captured her, declared her a spy, damn near caused her death in the dungeon...and now she held power over him and had promised not to use it.

Poor Andrew obviously didn't like being in her debt, and she chuckled about it all afternoon.

Supper was much the same as always, except Merrick spent his time speaking in a low voice to Gavin. She didn't mind; it gave her a chance to observe him. Her eyes skimmed over the silver at his temples, and she decided "not even two-score" years wasn't *that* old. Pearl had called him "twice her age" but Saffy was several years older. Surely, she and Merrick weren't *that* many years apart?

Why? What do ye care?

She frowned. She *didn't* care. It was mere curiosity. If Merrick wasn't so much older than her, then...

Then ye might no' feel wrong about lusting after him?

Lust? Was that what he was making her feel?

Aye, mayhap. He was a well-built man, and watching him train, or watching him stretch right after waking, or watching him bathe in the loch with his men...the sight of his body made her feel *warm*. And imagining touching him, touching his body, it made her *ache*.

She was no fool; she knew what it meant, and more than once had resented this ridiculous costume, because it meant she couldn't pull up her skirts and relieve the ache with her own fingers.

And sometimes, when he looked at her with that too-knowing gaze, she wondered what *he* was seeing.

"Saf!"

His call jerked her out of her reverie, and she jumped forward with the wine pitcher. But he waved her away.

"Nay. I'm retiring early."

She glanced at the arrow slits in the wall, surprised the sun hadn't set yet. "Aye," she agreed.

"Aye?" he prompted with a glare.

"Aye, Devil."

He growled.

She grinned.

"Merrick," Gavin began in a warning tone, but Merrick held up his hand to his second.

"I ken."

What had they been speaking of?

Merrick's gaze swept over his children, who were being surprisingly well-behaved. Usually they finished supping long before the adults and were ushered off to bed by Nell. Today, though, they all smiled cherubically at Merrick.

"Dinnae make me regret trusting ye all," he warned.

"Aye, Da," came a chorus of replies.

Mary nodded to her father, as if acknowledging his warning, but Andrew was strangely subdued. He glared at Saffy, but when Merrick's gaze landed on him, he flushed and turned his gaze to his trencher.

And Saffy didn't bother hiding her smirk, even as she trotted after Merrick, carefully balancing the pitcher of wine.

By the time he'd washed his face and hands, the sun was barely on the horizon. Instead of pulling back the cover on the bed, he settled in front of a small table in front of the window, which held a chessboard and a bowl of summer berries.

He picked up one of the tiny carved soldiers and rolled it idly between his fingers. "Do ye play, Saf?"

She looked up from where she was spreading out her pallet. "Chess? Aye."

His snort was unexpected. "Of course ye do. Pour two goblets and play me."

She raised her brows, but did as he commanded, settling herself in the chair opposite him. When she realized he was staring at her, she discovered she was sitting as a lady might—back straight, hands folded in her lap. Forcing herself to relax, she tried to mimic his easy slouch.

'Tis far more comfortable!

A small grin tugged at the corner of his lips as he nodded and placed the pawn back on the board. "Ye're sure ye ken the rules? We could play something simpler like Fox and Geese."

She'd found a carved board for the strategy game, along with one for Nine Man Morris, while straightening his trunk a few days ago. While both were easier games, she'd always enjoyed chess.

She shrugged. "Or Naughts and Crosses, if ye think the wine will loosen yer focus, milord?" Her smile was innocent—she was sure of it.

He glared, likely offended by her insinuation he couldn't handle the simplistic game. "Ye take the oak," he growled.

His pieces were carved from a dark-colored wood, while hers were light. His were smooth in her hand when she took one of his knights—the small man sitting tall on his horse—and she didn't bother hiding her smile of satisfaction.

Instead of moving one of his pieces, Merrick settled back in his chair and reached for his goblet. "Ye play well."

Had he sacrificed his knight to discover that about her? Her smile faded. "Ye've been playing recklessly," she shot.

His lips twitched again, but he lifted his wine. Once he'd finished swallowing, he shrugged. "With naught at risk, 'tisnae as much fun."

Her heart began to pound. "What would ye risk?"

"Secrets."

The quickness of his reply made her wonder if he'd been

planning this all along. Secrets? "One for every piece taken, I assume?"

He held her gaze as his chin dropped, and the *promise* in his eyes made her want to lick her lips.

Wagering secrets. It was a risk, indeed, especially because she had so much she couldn't tell him. But there was *much* she wanted to know about him: the stories of his children, his dead wives, his brothers...where her family's jewels were.

And ye are a verra, verra good chess player.

She grinned. "Aye, accepted."

He shot forward and immediately moved one of the soldiers—a pawn—and she countered with one of her own. He was right; the play *was* more exhilarating knowing what was at stake.

The clouds were a brilliant red on the horizon when he took her next piece, a pawn. It had been a sacrifice to get his castle into position, but she still shifted uncomfortably at his wolfish, expectant look as he settled back against his chair.

"Hmm." He rolled the pawn between his fingers. "A secret. What shall I ask..."

She swallowed and sat straighter, knowing what he would ask, and wondering how she could deflect the question.

"Who are yer people?" he asked directly. "Yer clan?"

She shook her head, then took a deep breath. "People who would nae like to ken I am here."

"Ye came without their permission?"

Her father's, at least. "Aye."

"Lindsays?" he snapped shrewdly, obviously hoping to catch her.

"Nay, I'm...from the Highlands," she said carefully.

He eyed her too-warm surcoat derisively. "Ye've told me no worthwhile secrets. Tell me of yer family."

She could do that, at least, without naming herself as a Sinclair or a laird's daughter.

"My father is doting, but understands duty. My older sister and younger sister have both been married. I have—I have a twin sister."

She said the last part tightly, surprised at the wave of emotion which crashed over her at thinking of Citrine and this mission they'd vowed to undertake. She hadn't sent word to her twin in over three sennights. Was Citrine worried? Was Da still ill?

"Citrine?" he asked quietly.

Her eyes snapped to his. "How—who told ye?"

He shrugged. "Ye speak in yer sleep sometimes, and 'tis a memorable name."

Aye, and dangerous if he connected it to the Sinclair Jewels. "'Tis a worthwhile secret," she said as she reached for her bishop.

As they took their turns, the tension slowly drained from her shoulders, and she found herself breathing easier and admiring his style of play. His hands were constantly occupied with the fallen pieces or the goblet, but he watched the board and her moves with a hawk-like glare. But rarely did he deliberate his own moves. Nay, it was as if he held a collection of options in his mind, and as soon as she made her own moves, he reacted with lightning speed.

He was swift and brutal and a worthy opponent, and there was only one way to play with someone like that: lure him into a position where each path required sacrifices.

She managed not to crow with glee when she eventually took his castle, but didn't bother hiding her smile.

His chin dipped in concession. "One secret," he said carelessly, his hand wrapped around the stem of the goblet.

And if she hadn't seen how white his knuckles were, she might've believed he was unconcerned.

Lifting her own goblet to her lips, she sipped at the sweet, dark wine and contemplated.

She could ask why his children all looked so different. She could ask if he had more children spread throughout Sutherland territory. But that wouldn't advance her mission here.

She could ask if he was aware his oldest daughter was in love with his youngest warrior. Knowing how Merrick felt about Mary, it would be sure to cause Andrew trouble, but as much as she wanted the lad to pay for his accusations, she knew that wouldn't help her either.

She wanted to know about *Merrick*. Wanted to know why they call him Devil. And there was one rumor she needed confirmed.

"Did ye kill yer brother?"

He was silent for a long moment, eying her from under hooded lids. Finally, he dipped his chin. "Aye."

"Why?"

Hooking his arm over the back of his chair, he shifted position slightly, and began to twist the goblet in his other hand. His attention drifted to the distant sunset, and he took a deep breath.

"My father and uncles had many children out of wedlock. Their father did as well. There are Sutherland bastards spread all over the Highlands, from what I've heard."

"And the Lowlands?"

A smile flashed as he glanced back at her. "Aye, John Lindsay's mother was the Lindsay laird's wild sister. He's older than me, so feels he should have a claim to my position."

She knew most of this already from listening to him speak to his seneschal, but was pleased to hear it directly. "But he's no' legitimate," she pointed out as she placed her goblet beside the chess board.

He shrugged. "He's one of dozens. I suppose he feels he has the right to challenge, because his mother was a laird's daughter."

"Outside the bonds of marriage..." She frowned as she

stood and crossed to the mantle, where she knew the flint was kept. "Ye're no' a bastard."

"Nay, but unless Lindsay wins his campaign, Willie is my heir, and *he's* a bastard."

"Unless ye marry again."

Her throat went dry as she considered the possibility. Why? Why did the thought of him marrying someone make her feel so uncomfortable?

Must be the wine.

Aye. That was it.

She concentrated on lighting the candle, then turned back to the table to find him frowning at her.

"Ye asked about Robbie," he reminded her.

She let out a breath. Aye, the dead brother. So why was her mind still lingering on the thought of him marrying?

MARRY AGAIN?

Why did the thought send a chill through him? He loved Willie, aye, but knew his son's illegitimacy would cause problems for the clan in years to come. He'd always known it'd be easier if he had a legitimate son, which is why he'd married Elizabeth, then Katharine.

Which is why, when neither of them bore a living child, he'd tried to form a marriage contract with one of the Sinclair Jewels.

But now…the thought of remarrying soured the wine on his tongue and in his stomach. He hoped to draw her—and his —attention away from the thought.

"Ye asked about Robbie."

When she eventually nodded and moved back to the board, the candle lit her face with a warm glow.

"Robbie was younger than me, but Da claimed him,"

Merrick began. "His mother was one of the kitchen servants, so I grew up with him underfoot. He was…different."

She placed the candle beside the board, then sat on the edge of her seat. "Different?"

"He lacked…" Merrick shook his head slightly, not sure how to describe it. "He would hurt animals sometimes, just to see what they would do. It wasnae bad when he was younger, but after Da died and I became laird, he was harder to control. He'd lash out and didnae seem to care he was hurting others." There was one thing Merrick had never been able to forgive. "He lacked control."

"So, ye killed him?" she asked, brows raised.

"More than once I'd wanted to, when his lack of under-standing or care caused harm to one of my men in battle, and he always managed to explain his shortcomings…but nay." He shook his head, then took a deep breath. "'Tis no' why I killed him."

She didn't speak, just stared at him with those brilliant eyes with interest.

"I'd heard rumors about his lasses, how they hadnae always been willing. But nae one was eager to speak against him. Then one day…"

He swallowed and shook his head, the memory of that rainy afternoon creeping back into his mind, chilling him.

"One day I found him with Mary. She was barely twelve and was fighting him, but he had her skirts up already."

He doubted Saf was aware of the way her hand rose to her throat, horror in her expression. It was a thoroughly feminine reaction, but he couldn't appreciate it right now.

"His own niece?" she choked out.

It was a struggle to keep the memory of that failure, that *disgust*, from sweeping over him. "I didnae give him the chance to talk his way out of it. I slit his throat, then held Mary as she cried."

He'd cried right along with her and begged her forgiveness, but had never told anyone that.

It was a long moment before he realized he was staring at the candle flame. He squeezed his eyes shut, then took a breath, and forced a nonchalant mien when he faced her once more.

Only to discover her watching him with a look he couldn't identify.

Finally, she nodded firmly. "Good."

Approval.

She *approved* of his actions? He'd cut his own brother down in cold blood, and she'd approved.

What a surprising lass.

Play began again, more subdued, but he was distracted. The wine held no more interest as he considered his opponent more carefully. She took the next few pieces, but it was as if his story had bothered her, because her questions were easier, less intrusive.

What were yer wives' names?

Tell me about yer father.

Do ye remember yer grandmother?

What's yer favorite dish?

He answered them quickly, carelessly, thankful they were simple, and responded in kind.

The stars were out when he realized she's maneuvered him into a corner. He could take her queen—which he saw now she'd sacrificed—but her bishop would take his king. It was the only option, which meant his question would have to be a good one if he was going to have any hope winning secrets from her as Gavin had suggested at supper.

Slowly, he reached across the table and moved his piece to take her queen, leaving his king undefended. Deliberately taking his time, he propped his elbows on the table and rolled the queen between his palms, staring at her.

There was really only one question he needed to hear the answer to.

"Ye swear to me ye're no' a Lindsay? No' here at his behest?"

She shifted forward and mirrored his pose.

"Merrick, I swear it on my mother's grave. I'm no' spying for him."

It was the first time he'd heard her use his name. Sometimes she'd called him *milord*, but mostly it was *Devil* or *Sutherland*.

Hearing his name on her lips was strangely…*intense*.

What would she look like in a gown? Her cropped hair perfumed and pinned? If she smiled at him, not in triumph or teasing, but in encouragement? As if she *wanted* him.

He swallowed, feeling himself harden beneath his kilt.

Best remind himself of her purpose here. "Ye're still a spy, though?"

She didn't reply, but held his gaze.

Cursing himself, he brought the queen to his lips, sliding the smoother oak across the sensitive skin and staring at her mouth. Aye, it worked; her lips parted on a slight gasp and her eyes widened.

She might not know it, but she desired him as much as he desired her.

"Why are ye here, Saf?" he asked in a low voice, willing her to tell him.

Mayhap he'd pushed her too hard, because she straightened quickly and reached for her bishop.

She hadn't answered his question!

His hand darted out and closed around her wrist, stopping her. Under his fingers, her pulse pounded, telling him her reaction to him—or his question—was nowhere near calm.

Slowly, he dragged her hand toward him, until he was holding her fingers in his. That warmth made his arm tingle, and he noted she made no move to pull away, even if she didn't meet his eyes.

"Answer me, Saf. Why are ye here?"

With her other hand, she used her bishop to knock over his king. Then she looked up. "To find something," she finally said softly.

And when he squeezed her hand, he could swear she squeezed his back.

Aye, she'd found something, and so had he.

CHAPTER 7

Saffy had never been completely comfortable on horseback.

Oh, she could list diseases of the horse, and how to care for them, and what the best riding techniques were…but actually getting *on* one was a different story.

Still, when Merrick came to her the day after their chess match and told her she'd be going with him and his men on patrol to look for Lindsay, she didn't argue. It was the first time since she'd been in the keep that Gavin had found evidence of Lindsay's raiders, and she was excited to be part of it.

It wasn't until she was mounted up and riding with the men—concentrating fully on not falling off—that she thought to wonder why.

Because of what she'd learned about Lindsay? She wanted to help defeat him?

Or because she wanted to prove to Merrick she wasn't a spy for his brother?

Last night, he'd asked her why she was on Sutherland land. She hadn't been able to tell him—she knew how dangerous it could be to her mission. It wasn't that she didn't trust him. She suspected he was a good man, and the rumors of him being a devil were mostly exaggerations. His story about his brother Robbie's death was a good example.

But she didn't trust him not to put the good of his own clan above her mission to find the jewels, and if his clan was implicated in a theft of some sort, she couldn't guess what he'd do.

Nay, it was better to keep up her disguise, and keep her mission a secret.

She'd found no evidence of the jewels so far, nor any history or tales which would indicate their hiding place was known. So, for now, she'd keep looking, and do her best to make Merrick trust her.

Gavin led their little band unerringly. She rode behind Merrick and beside Andrew, who didn't speak to her at all. There were ten others in their group, all warriors armed and ready.

She saw nothing suspicious. The day was beautiful, the sun was bright overhead, and her stomach was tight with anticipation. Or excitement. Or just happiness because he'd shared so much with her last night.

Her mind wandered, thinking back on the stories they'd shared, mostly innocuous…and the way his hand had felt in hers.

He'd held her hand! She was no fool; she knew men had close friendships, the same as women. But the way he'd touched her, the way he'd squeezed her hand…it had been hard to remember he thought her a lad.

He…he *did* still think of her as a lad, aye?

She was frowning—her thighs already aching from the effort it took to stay atop the horse—when Gavin led them across a small stream. They were several hours from the keep by that point, and the terrain was rockier. In fact, the path they were on would lead them directly between a rock over-hang and a tremendous boulder.

It would be a perfect place for an ambush.

But what did she know? She was a scholar, not a warrior.

Still, the closer they got, the more uncomfortable she was. As Gavin led Merrick through the pass, she worked up the courage to say something.

"Andrew, should we—"

That was as far as she got before the attack came.

With blood-curdling cries, the warriors attacked from either side of the hidden pass. Gavin went down, and Merrick whirled, his sword appearing in his hand as he hacked his way toward his friend.

As Saffy froze, forgetting how to breathe, the rest of the Sutherland warriors let loose battle cries and joined the fray.

"Saf!"

It was Merrick yelling her name, which broke her trance. He was probably livid his squire wasn't beside him, helping him fight.

She scrambled for the sword at her waist, cursing her sweat-dampened palms and wondering how in the world she was supposed to remember the few moves he and Citrine had taught her.

Her blade in her hand now, she kicked her horse into motion, and bless him, but he was obviously better trained for battle than she was. When one of their attackers—wearing a plaid she didn't recognize—loomed over her, his sword raised, her horse swung out of his path, even as she ducked stupidly.

Sweet Virgin, ye're going to die! Citrine is the warrior, no' ye!

Her mind was *not* being helpful.

If Citrine could do this, *she* could. Merrick was counting on her.

Ahead, he was whirling and slicing, a blade in each hand as he controlled his horse with his powerful thighs.

'Tis a hell of a time to notice his thighs, Saffy.

An enemy—they must be Lindsays!—lunged for his rear, but before she could shout a warning, Merrick had thrown himself sideways and stabbed upward, catching the man in the gut.

Saffy remembered to inhale and yanked her horse's head toward Merrick. She didn't know what use she'd be to him, but couldn't bear the thought of him being wounded.

"*Saf!*" he bellowed again.

Apparently, he thought she should be by his side as well.

Time sped up again as her animal wove its way between the clumps of fighters, and she kept her attention on Merrick, swallowing down her terror at the screams of pain and clashes of metal.

She would reach him. She had to.

And she would've, had Andrew not stumbled in front of her horse then, defending himself from a much larger Lindsay warrior who landed blow after blow on the weakening young man.

Saffy knew she couldn't allow Andrew to be hurt, not when she could help. Merrick might've wanted her by his side, but surely he'd rather know Andrew was safe?

Her mind made up, she took a deep breath as the battling pair passed to her left, then raised herself in her stirrups.

With a battle cry which would've made Citrine proud, she threw herself out of her saddle toward the Lindsay warrior.

WHEN HE SAW Saf throw herself off the horse, Merrick went a little mad.

It had been bad enough knowing he'd ridden right into an ambush. What the hell had Gavin been thinking, to lead them this way? Merrick had already been frowning as he followed his friend, knowing this pass was a dangerous spot...but he'd trusted Gavin not to be so stupid.

Then, when the Lindsays had attacked, there'd been a moment of elation. Aye, he and his men were under attack...but he *finally* had the chance to engage his brother face-to-face!

It was long moments before he realized John wasn't with his men.

And a few very *short* moments before Merrick realized Saf was in danger as well.

He'd yelled her name, but the lass had just sat there, staring wide-eyed and terrified at the battle around her. He'd begun fighting his way toward her then, no longer caring about the Lindsays, or John, or even the fact that Gavin's forehead was bleeding.

He was only thinking about reaching her.

Holding her.

Kissing her.

Ensuring she was safe.

It was hard to keep an eye on her with the battle raging around him, but he continued to fight his way toward her. His horse was well-trained, as was hers. Despite the scent of blood and the screams in the air, her animal wouldn't panic.

And then, thank God, she'd drew her sword and began to move toward him, and he knew she was at least able to function. He'd be able to reach her and keep her safe.

Aye, everything was looking up...right until the daft lass threw herself off her horse.

Merrick had shouted her name again, just as she slammed into the back of a Lindsay warrior, her short sword plunging into the man's back up to its hilt. She rode the body to the ground, only to be snatched up by the hood of her surcoat by an *extremely* angry-looking Andrew.

Angry she'd interfered with his battle, or angry that she'd saved him?

Merrick fended off another attack, irate the Lindsays seemed to be focusing on him, keeping him from her side.

Still, as his men cut the attackers down, he watched Saf. She stood back-to-back with Andrew, doing her best to fend off blows with her large dirk. Darting forward and back, she slashed and stabbed, incapacitating at least two Lindsays who'd underestimated her abilities.

Despite the danger all around, Merrick found himself smiling grimly.

I taught her that move.

Finally, his last attacker lay dead at his feet, and Merrick whirled to take stock. Gavin was sitting on the ground, holding his head—in pain or shame? The rest of his men were standing, or finishing off their opponents…

Except for Andrew. He was still locked in combat with a Lindsay warrior. As Andrew spun out of the way, Saf darted in to take his place. But before she could attack, the tip of the man's sword sliced across her forearm.

Blood bloomed from the wound, and her face paled as she stumbled to the side.

Before Merrick could move, Andrew had lunged back into position and thrust his sword deep into the enemy's unprotected neck.

Just like that, the battle was finished, the Lindsays defeated.

But as much as he wanted to rail against Gavin, or to hold Saf and ensure she was safe, he needed to be the Sutherland Devil first.

"Farran!" he barked, singling out Gavin's second. "Lead the retreat. Each man pair with a wounded comrade. Let no Sutherland fall behind!"

Then, because he knew it was expected, he swung his bloodied sword in a circle over his head. "Without fear!"

His warriors—even the wounded—screamed the clan's words back. "*Without fear!*"

Farran pulled Gavin up behind him, and turned his horse to gallop toward the distant keep. Others helped friends up or began to wrap wounds.

Merrick turned his horse toward Andrew and Saf.

His former squire was bent over Saf's arm, clearly trying to check the wound, but she kept pulling back. Finally, Andrew sighed and swung up on his horse, then offered her his hand.

Merrick reached them before Saf could reach for the lad. "Go, Andrew," he commanded in a stern voice. "Ride in the rear and watch for stragglers."

Andrew's eyes darted between his laird and Saf, and Merrick could see he wanted to argue. Finally, he lowered his chin in acceptance.

"Ye saved my life, Saf," the young warrior choked out.

"Aye," she croaked, her face still pale. "Twice."

Andrew held her gaze. "I'm sorry I doubted ye."

Merrick could tell Saf was in no condition to stand around and talk, and *he* was in no mood to allow Andrew to continue ignoring his orders. "*Andrew!*"

The young man yanked his horse around and galloped for home.

Alone now, Merrick took a deep breath and looked to Saf.

She seemed so tiny and vulnerable, clutching her right forearm to her chest. Blood stained her sleeve and the front of the surcoat, but it wasn't so much he was worried about her passing out. Nay, it was *fear* which had her pale and shaking now.

With a muttered curse, he leaned down, grabbed her under her arms, and pulled her into his lap. He wrapped one arm around her, tucked her against his chest, and kicked his horse after his men.

Miles had gone by before he heard her say something.

They were safe enough now, beyond the reach of the Lindsays and in the open. He knew his men were on their way back to the keep.

He could afford a few moments to set his heart at ease.

Yanking the horse's reins, he turned the animal toward a stream, thinking only to allow Saf a drink, and maybe check her wound.

"What did ye say?" he asked gruffly.

She pulled away from his chest, where she'd been snuggling. "I said, I left my sword there."

The image of her jumping off her horse, the flash of her blade as she plunged it into the Lindsay's back, slammed into him once more. He stiffened, unconsciously tightening his hold on her.

"Ye're hurting me."

Hurting her? When they reached the stream, he pulled the horse to a stop and swung his leg over, without loosening his hold.

Hurting *her?*

Carefully, he let her legs drop until she was supporting herself, then forced himself to step back, before he exploded at her.

"Hurting ye?" he repeated in a deceptively quiet tone. "Hurting *ye?*"

Her chin rose, and she met his hard gaze. "Aye, but now my arm hurts more."

"*Hurting ye!* Do ye have *any idea* how much pain ye would've caused had more than just yer arm been injured? Did ye even stop to *think* afore ye threw yerself from yer horse?"

So much for his control. He scrubbed both hands through his hair. "Ye could've been wounded much worse, Saf! Ye could've been *killed!*'

Her eyes rounded, and her mouth made a little "oh" of

surprise. Thank God, she was finally understanding what danger she'd been in!

But then she took a deep breath and ruined his relief.

"Would that have bothered ye, Merrick, had I been killed?"

It would have broken me, lass.

The thought—the sudden realization—was more than he was willing to admit. He'd known her such a short time!

But it was the truth. Knowing she'd been hurt had caused *him* pain. If she'd been killed…

"*God's wounds*, Saf," he growled, reaching for her.

He pulled her against his chest, one hand splayed across her back, and the other cupping her hip, then crushed his lips down over hers. He swallowed the adorable little noise of surprise she made, and let his body show her how much she'd come to mean to him.

He knew the moment she relaxed from her shock and moved under him. Her uninjured hand turned against his chest, and she traced circles on his skin, which just made him moan again. She matched him with a little whimper, and when his tongue pressed against her lips, she invited him in.

God's wounds.

When did the lass learn to kiss? Merrick couldn't complain. With her pressed against him like this, despite the danger, he felt himself hardening. He wanted nothing more than to lay her down beside the stream, peel off that ridiculous disguise, and love her the way a woman should be loved.

But he couldn't. She wasn't ready for it, and he… It had been too long to start now.

She kissed like a woman who knew what she wanted, and he desperately wanted to give it to her.

Maybe one day he would.

With a groan, he pulled away from her, and when her lips followed him, he almost gave in.

Instead, he pressed his forehead against hers, panting.

Her eyes were open, and she ground her pelvis against his.

He tightened his hold on her and on his control. "Easy, lass."

That was what did it. With a gasp, she reared back, jerking away from him. "*Lass?*" she repeated.

He straightened, and when he saw her incredulous expression, he began to chuckle.

"Aye, *lass*. I'd no' kiss a *lad* the way I just kissed ye."

She opened her mouth, but no sound came out. Finally, her shaking fingers lifted to her lips.

"How long?" she whispered.

His expression softened, and using his hold on her hips, pulled her closer. "Since the first, Saf. I held ye that night, and I kenned it," he admitted gently.

"Ye knew I was a—a lass? Ye've been teaching me, and treating me like a…like yer squire."

"Aye." He nodded. "I wanted to get close to ye, to make ye trust me."

He carefully pulled her injured forearm away from her body and turned it over, examining the wound. It appeared clean, and although she would need stitches, it would likely heal well.

"And once I trusted ye?"

Still holding her, he met her eyes. She was staring at him with the most serious expression.

"Do ye?" he whispered. "Trust me?"

"Do ye trust me?" she fired back.

It took a long moment for him to admit the truth. "Last night ye swore ye weren't Lindsay's spy. Today I saw ye risk yer life"—he wiggled her wounded forearm—"to kill Lindsay's men. I dinnae think ye're one of them anymore."

"I never was."

"Aye, 'tis what ye've been saying all along. I dinnae ken why ye came to my land…"

He twined his fingers through hers and pressed her hips against him once more. They still had several hours of riding ahead of them. He needed to cleanse her wound to ensure it wouldn't fester before the healer could tend to it. He needed to deal with Gavin and the other injured men and determine what to do next when it came to Lindsay.

Aye, he had plenty he should be considering. But standing here beside this stream, his lips still tingling from her kiss, and his skin still tingling from her nearness, there was only one thing on his mind.

I dinnae ken why ye came to my land...

"But now that ye're here, I'm no' letting ye go."

It was a vow.

CHAPTER 8

I'm no' letting ye go.

Saffy couldn't decide if it was a threat or not. Still, when he kissed her again, hard and desperate, she decided she didn't care. Being in Merrick's arms made her forget everything else.

Especially insignificant concerns like *he'd known she was a lass.*

But if it resulted in her being pressed against him like this, his tongue caressing her lips, she couldn't be *too* irritated that her disguise wasn't as good as she'd hoped.

After, he pulled her toward the stream and washed her wound, his hands gentle, even if he didn't meet her eyes or say a word. Then he lifted her up on his horse, cradling her on his lap as he nudged the animal toward home.

Nestled against his chest, Saffy gave a secret smile when she felt his hardness pressed against her bottom. She knew what *that* meant, and couldn't help her little wiggle of excitement.

She'd accepted that she was attracted to the man, but had bemoaned ever doing anything about it. But now it turned out not only did he know she was a woman; he was *attracted* to her as well. So, who was to say he wouldn't do more than kiss her? Was he taking her to his chambers right now? Would he peel her clothing off and lick her skin the way she wanted him to?

Her breaths were coming faster, and she wiggled again, unconsciously trying to ease the ache between her legs.

"Stop that," he growled, tightening his hold on her.

She froze, then realized what he was objecting to as his member gave another jump under his kilt. A small smile tugged at her lips.

"Aye, Devil," she agreed in a teasing tone, her cheek against his chest.

Her arm burned, her pulse thrummed, and she was certain his *I'm no' letting ye go* had been a promise of further pleasure. But despite everything buzzing through her head, she fell asleep.

When they reached the keep, she was startled awake. To her surprise, Merrick seemed to ignore her all together, or at least treat her no different than he had Saf, his squire. He swung her down from his horse before she was even fully awake, then strode into the great hall, bellowing orders and questions.

She scurried in behind him, trying to figure out what he was thinking.

It soon became apparent that, no matter what they'd shared by the stream, no matter his intense, choked whisper when he'd pressed his forehead to hers and made that vow, he was now thinking of his clan.

None were dead, and of them, Gavin seemed to be the most seriously wounded. His cut had stopped bleeding, but Farran had to support him completely, and he didn't seem to be fully conscious.

Gavin might've been Merrick's friend, but it was the Sutherland Devil who demanded a reckoning as they waited for the healer to arrive.

And he might've tried to hide it, but Saffy could see how alarmed Merrick was when Gavin couldn't answer for his failure.

The healer—a beautiful older woman named Magda—lived in the village but kept a fully-stocked healing room in the keep. Enlisting a few of the maids, she moved among the men, stitching and bandaging and offering light-hearted banter to keep spirits up.

She checked Andrew, who was unharmed thanks to Saffy, then moved on to Saffy. The older woman gestured to the surcoat.

"Well, lad, let's have that smelly thing off, shall we? One of the lasses will have it washed up, if ye persist in wearing it."

Reluctantly, Saffy began to pull the heavy wool from her shoulders, feeling as if she were removing armor. Merrick knew her for who she really was, so why was she still hiding?

Because he does no' ken who ye really are.

Magda clucked impatiently, but her hands were careful as she helped pull material over Saffy's wound. The healer's eyes rested briefly on Saffy's chest where the linen shirt hid the wrapping over her breasts.

Was it Saffy's imagination, or had Magda winked before leaning over her sword wound?

She might've continued that line of thought had the healer not chosen that moment to prod at the deep gash. Everything went white-hot then, and Saffy was sure her whimper was pitiful.

And maybe she would've screamed, except at that moment, a heavy hand came down on her shoulder. She glanced up to see Merrick standing beside her, his attention on his men spread throughout the hall.

But his thumb was making tiny circles against the linen of her shirt, as if offering support. And that, more than anything else, *relaxed* her.

She turned her attention back to the healer and tried to pretend—as he was—that Merrick's attention was no more than a laird to his squire. But it didn't stop the spread of warmth throughout her.

It seemed like forever before Magda declared her wound treated, stitched, and wrapped sufficiently.

The healer sighed in contentment and sat back. "Ye'll have a scar, but a young warrior like yerself shouldnae mind, aye?" That was *definitely* a wink. Maybe she just winked at all her charges? "But I heard it was bravely got, defending someone ye might no' have had reason to."

Saffy's gaze darted across the hall to rest on Andrew, who was clutching a mug of ale and glaring broodingly in their direction.

Magda nodded. "Aye, young Andrew has already told the story. Ye saved his life, Saf, and the laird will no' forget that."

They both glanced up at Merrick, who didn't respond, or even look their way. But his fingers did tighten briefly on Saffy's shoulder, which might've been an agreement.

She cleared her throat and lowered her chin. "I only did what anyone would do for—for a fellow warrior." The words felt dry in her mouth.

Magda chuckled as she folded up her linen bandages. "But would they do it for a man who'd accused them of treachery, thrown them in the dungeon, and left them to die?"

Saffy recognized the teasing and couldn't resist quipping back. "They might, were they as good and selfless as I am."

Miracle of miracles, Merrick snorted at that, obviously not ignoring them as thoroughly as he appeared to be.

Giving up on his charade, he pierced the healer with a glare. "Are ye done here, Magda?"

"Aye, milord," the woman said, rising to her feet and bobbing in deference. "I've given my leave to most of yer men to return home. I'll visit over the coming days. Gavin will need to stay in the healing room, and I'll sit with him in between. I can change wee Saf's bandage as well."

Merrick nodded, a Devil once more. Then, using his hold on Saffy's shoulder, he tugged her to her feet. "He'll stay in my chambers, and I'll alert ye to any change."

The healer bobbed again in agreement, but Merrick was already pulling Saffy toward the stairs.

He? Merrick had called her "he". Saffy shook her head, not sure if she was confused or lightheaded or just exhausted. Did Merrick *want* her to remain Saf, his squire? Or…

She stumbled over her own feet, and before she knew it, Merrick had swept her up into his arms. Why was he still treating her like his squire?

In his chambers, he kicked the door closed and stomped toward the bed. She half-expected him to toss her on the mattress judging by how tense his shoulders were. But instead, he lowered her gently, not meeting her eyes.

When he reached for her feet, she almost pulled them out of his reach, but then relaxed and remembered he knew her secret.

Well, one of them, at least.

That thought kept her occupied as he tugged her shoes off, pulled back the coverlet, and pushed her legs under. But when he reached for the tie of her shirt at her neck, she sucked in a breath.

Was this…was this what she hoped? His knuckles brushed against her skin, and she damn near moaned in anticipation.

Why wasn't he looking at her? He was frowning as he studied the cords, then made a sound of satisfaction when they popped free.

She wanted to echo it, and maybe she would've, except he distracted her by tugging her shirt up and over her head, leaving her sitting in his bed wearing only her breeches and the bindings around her breasts.

At last!

But nay, he only fisted his hand around the linen and stepped back.

His pale eyes finally met hers, and although half-dazed with desire and exhaustion, she thought she saw wariness in them. "I'll take—I'll have this stitched and washed with yer surcoat," he offered.

She opened her mouth to repeat *"washed?"* incredulously, but all that emerged was a croak. He'd removed her clothes, he'd kissed her, and now he was leaving her alone?

He cleared his throat. "I'll bring ye food. For now, rest."

At that command, he spun on his heel and stomped to the door. Once he was gone, Saffy found herself sinking to the pillows.

She was a scholar. She didn't like being confused.

Did he or did he not feel the same desire she felt for him? His reaction to her closeness indicated he did, so why wasn't he acting on it? Mayhap he was concerned for her? But he had no reason to think she was anyone other than a free woman without ties, who knew her own mind.

She closed her eyes on a sigh, hating this uncertainty, and hating the Lindsay who'd stabbed her just as much.

Today she'd experienced her first battle—and handled herself fairly well, if she did say so herself—and her first painful wound. She'd also experienced her first kiss, which she liked much more.

But despite the way her mind was whirling, exhaustion won out, and she found herself following her laird's command to rest.

It was hours later when she felt the bed dip beside her, and she instinctively rolled toward the newcomer, part of her thinking it was Citrine.

But nay, the arms which wrapped around her were much stronger and larger than her sister, and the scent of leather and smoke was different—better—than anything she'd smelled before.

Still half-asleep, she tucked herself under his chin, her injured arm curled between them. She wanted to kiss him again.

They lay like that for long moments, her listening to his heartbeat, wondering if he was there to make love to her…but sleep crept in once more.

His breathing lulled her, and his arms held her as if she were actually important to him.

I'm no' letting ye go.

She fell asleep smiling.

Mayhap another bastard wouldnae be that bad.

Merrick slouched at the head table, his untouched trencher before him, and the noise of the meal swirling around him, staring into his flagon of ale. It was the day after the battle with the Lindsays, and nothing had changed; Andrew was still sulking, Gavin was still unconscious, and Saf…

Saf was still half-naked in his bed.

She'd woken with him this morning and had stared with bright eyes at his rock-hard cock before he'd reached for his kilt. It hadn't been fear or disgust he'd seen in her expression, nay. It'd been *want*, the same want that had been coursing through him for days now.

That kiss didnae make aught better, fool.

Cursing himself, he took a draught of the ale, wondering if he should've eaten something first. Was he *trying* to get drunk?

A squeal from the other end of the table caught his attention, and he lunged forward in time to catch the roll Maggie had lobbed at Adelaide. When he glared at the wild twelve-year-old, Maggie paled and sank back into her seat.

Beside him, Mary chuckled low in her throat and leaned over to pluck the bread from his hand. Still clutching the goblet, he turned his glare on her, but she merely patted his arm and took a bite of the bread.

"Ye're no' fit company this afternoon, Da."

"Aye," he growled, collapsing back in his seat.

"And ye're getting drunk, which isnae good. Are ye feeling guilty?"

Why? he wanted to snap. This daughter of his was perceptive. He raised a brow in her direction, and her lips twitched.

"Well, *I* dinnae ken why any of ye brave warriors would feel guilty, but Andrew's been moping about, too."

"He's feeling guilty because he needed to be saved by a—a lad."

He'd almost blurted Saf's secret. Last night, he'd treated her as his squire, as they'd been before she'd thrown herself off a horse to protect one of his warriors. Before he'd kissed her.

I'm no' ready to reveal her secret.

And he vowed to himself he'd discover *why* she'd come to his home dressed as a lad in the first place.

But Mary was shaking her head. "Nay, he's feeling guilty because Saf had every reason to want him dead, but instead she—I mean *he*—saved Andrew."

Merrick's eyes darted up to his daughter's, who didn't look at all uncomfortable by her slip. Had it been a slip? Or intentional?

He frowned, wondering who else had seen through Saf's disguise.

"Da, I stopped by to chat with Saf today. He said ye've locked him in and commanded him to rest."

She wasn't asking, but he nodded. "He lost a lot of blood," he mumbled, looking into his flagon once more.

Mary made a little noise of dismissal. "He's lonely, Da. And ye're terrible company. I'll sit in yer chair and glare at the bairns, if ye'd like, so ye can retire."

"Is that what I've been doing?"

She frowned fiercely, obviously an attempt to mimic him. "Aye," she growled in a low voice. "Ye're giving everyone indigestion."

With a snort, he slammed the flagon to the table. "And here's me thinking mayhap another bairn wouldnae be so bad. I cannae stand the sass I get from the ones I've already got!"

Mary leaned over and placed a gentle kiss on his cheek. "I ken what ye were thinking, Da, and I ken ye deserve to be happy. If another bairn would do that, then ye have my blessing."

Merrick was frowning slightly as he pulled away and stood up. He stared at his eldest child for a long moment, trying to understand her words. She just smiled sweetly and turned to Beck, who was trying to pick his nose with his knife.

I ken what ye were thinking.

Did she? Could his daughter guess how much he lusted after his own squire?

His frowned deepened. The fact that his sweet girl knew anything about a man's lust was a sin laid at Robbie's feet, and his brother was already burning in hell for it.

With a stifled sigh, Merrick turned from the table. Mary was right; he *was* unfit company.

And the fact he was trying to convince himself having another bastard might be nice was enough of a hint he was in desperate need of release. He needed to take himself in hand, the way he'd tried that night with Saf sleeping at his bedside. Mayhap he could find some privacy in his solar.

Aye, that was what he needed. A quick release, and he'd remember why taking Saf to bed would be a bad idea.

But his traitorous feet took him toward his own chamber, and when he pushed open the door, he sucked in a breath. She'd whirled from where she stood at the table, the chess board spread before her. The late-afternoon light coming through the window had turned her short hair honey-blonde, and he liked the way her eyes lit up to see him. She was wearing one of his shirts over her breeches, and the sleeves were rolled up to reveal one slim arm.

The reminder of her risk caused him to scowl.

"Ah," she drawled. "There's the Devil I was expecting."

He reached out and slammed the door closed. "Why are ye out of bed?"

"Because I was bored. And with no one to join me, there was naught to do."

The twinkle in her eyes told him she knew *exactly* what she was hinting at. And curse his traitorous cock.

He stalked toward her. "Who are ye?" he breathed, coming to a stop in front of her, his eyes raking her face. "Ye're no' a spy. A whore?"

"Is that what ye call any woman who enjoys a man's company? One who kens her own mind?"

He blew out an exasperated breath and ran his hand through his hair. What kind of idiot turned down an offer like Saf's?

One who has enough bastards.

But he didn't back up fast enough. She stepped closer and placed her hand on his chest. "I'll stop teasing ye, Merrick. Only tell me this, ye didnae plan to kiss me yesterday, did ye?"

"Nay," he growled. "No' at all. Ye might no' be a spy, but ye've been keeping secrets from me."

She nodded, as if he'd told her something she'd already known. Was she thinking about what he'd revealed there beside the stream? That her death would've mattered to him?

Would've *broken* him.

Before she could pull away, he grabbed her hand, the one resting against his chest, and turned it over. This was her right hand, the uninjured arm. His forefinger traced the fresh calluses she'd earned from training with him over the last weeks, but there were others…

"This is from a stylus," he said, remembering that first night in his chamber, when he'd examined her and wondered who she was. "Ye're no crofter."

She tugged her hand away, but he refused to let her go. When she tried to avoid his gaze, he made a warning sound deep in his throat.

"Who are ye, Saf?"

She was staring at his chin, and he watched her swallow.

"I— My sister tried to teach me to wield a sword, but I preferred working in my father's solar, reading the clan histories."

A lady. She was a lady, but not a Lindsay.

"God's wounds, Saf," he whispered hoarsely. "Yer father could be looking for ye even now!"

She shook her head slightly, her expression looking panicked. "He's no'. He doesnae ken—"

Merrick tried to keep his breathing even, tried to trust her. But the thought of Mary alone in another keep, without knowing where she was… He squeezed Saf's hand. "Who are ye?"

She met his eyes and shook her head. "I cannae, Devil."

And damn her eyes, but she sounded *apologetic*. He dropped her hand and stepped back. "Why?" he snarled. "Because ye do nae trust me?"

"Aye," she said sadly. "Because I ken ye are a good man, and if ye ken my family, ye'd send me back to them."

"And ye dinnae want to go?"

"Nay…" She swallowed. "I miss them terribly. But I came here for a reason."

"Which ye willnae tell me."

She didn't answer, just stared at him with sadness in those big blue eyes.

He cursed himself for a fool and strode for the door. He was keeping her secret for her, but she wasn't trusting him. He needed a good fight, another drink, and a quick release.

And at this point, he didn't care how he got them.

CHAPTER 9

Mayhap she should have told him who she was.

Merrick's bad mood lasted for days, and Saf knew she was partially responsible. Aye, there'd been no word from Lindsay, and aye, Gavin was still too faint for a reckoning from Merrick. In fact, the Sutherland second—poor man—couldn't sit up for long and would become dazed within a few words whenever Merrick confronted him. But Saf suspected there was more to Merrick's temper, because the easy camaraderie they'd built over the last weeks was gone.

She still served him meals, still trained with him, but he no longer singled her out. Her arm had healed well enough, although she was careful not to jostle it until Magda told her the stitches were ready to come out.

But Saffy hadn't moved out of Merrick's bed. She supposed it was a quiet sort of rebellion, forcing him to command her to leave.

He hadn't yet.

Every night, they performed her ablutions in silence, and she did her best to remind him she was a woman. Last night, she removed her shirt, unwound her breasts while standing at the table, and pulled her shirt back on. When she'd turned around, Merrick had been staring at her, breathing heavily.

And as she'd done every night since the battle with the Lindsays, she crawled into his bed and waited. And as he'd done every night, he stood there in the darkness, obviously debating with himself, before cursing under his breath, crawling in beside her, and hauling her up against him.

This morning she'd woken with his hands cupping her breast and his hard member nestling against her rear end. The intimacy had sent a spike of warmth straight to the secret area between her legs, and she'd smiled and pretended to stretch as she pushed back against him.

"God's wounds, Saf," he'd hissed as he jerked away from her and rolled out of bed. "Ye're making this too hard."

This?

She'd had to stifle her laughter as she watched him wind his kilt around himself—and his jutting erection. He'd done a good job of hiding what she most wanted to see, and she still wasn't sure why.

But that didn't mean she couldn't continue to tease him.

Of course, outside of his chamber, and in the clan's eyes, she was still just his squire. He was keeping her secret, despite her refusal to answer his questions. She decided that had to be the noblest thing she'd ever experienced, and it made her feel even worse about not trusting him with the truth.

But he was the Sutherland Devil. He'd once been engaged to marry Saffy's youngest sister. Pearl had broken that contract because she'd refused to leave Sinclair land, and had later realized a deep and abiding love for one of Da's warriors. But that hadn't helped Merrick, and until Saf understood his feelings about that broken betrothal, she couldn't risk telling him her real name.

Or why she was here.

Since she'd recovered enough for Merrick to allow her out

of his chamber—although she was sure had she really been a lad, he would've given her permission a day earlier—she'd finished examining the tapestries. No references to the Sinclairs were found. She'd spoken to the seneschal and a few of the elders, too, keeping her questions as innocuous as possible.

Whereas a fortnight before, the Sutherlands would've reacted with suspicion to her questions, now they were answered freely. Many of the clan knew of her actions in the battle with the Lindsays, and more than a few approached her to apologize for thinking her a spy.

Apparently, despite Andrew's embarrassment, he hadn't hesitated to tell everyone of her...well, she was hearing it called a "brave deed," and although she appreciated the praise, she secretly agreed with Merrick that it had been idiotic to put herself in so much danger.

But when she saw the way Mary smiled at Andrew, Saffy knew she'd save the lad's life again, if called on to do it.

Although she didn't mind making him squirm in apology.

"Where in the hell is Andrew?"

Merrick's question, roared in exasperation, jerked Saffy out of her thoughts. She was sitting in the afternoon shade as the laird trained with his most experienced warriors, and hadn't expected Andrew to be there.

Judging from the confused look Farran shot her way—as if asking her if *she* knew what was irritating the laird so much— he hadn't either. "Milord, Andrew hasnae trained with us afore. He was here this morning with the rest—"

With a growl, Merrick sheathed his sword. "If he ever wants to reach your level of skill, he should be here whenever he can."

There was nothing Farran could say in reply, so he merely bowed his head in agreement. Saffy frowned, wondering why Merrick was taking his anger out on

Andrew in particular. Or was he just frustrated at the stalemate with the Lindsays?

Or with her?

When he stalked past her, she leapt to her feet to offer him a drink from the skin of water she carried. He tossed her his weapon and drank from the skin as he walked.

She tried not to notice the way the drops ran down his chin and dripped onto his chest.

Ye're noticing, lass.

She swallowed and tried for levity as she hurried to catch up. "For an auld man, ye certainly can run."

He didn't slow as he headed toward the courtyard. "And for a *lad*, ye certainly dinnae move fast enough."

She chuckled as she caught up to him. "I'm twenty-two, ye ken."

That stopped him. He whirled so suddenly, she almost ran into him. Although she'd rather be pressed up against him, she shuffled back so she could tilt her head and meet his gaze.

"Truly?" he finally asked.

She nodded.

He slowly exhaled, his eyes difficult to read. "As a lad, ye looked younger than Willie, but I thought ye closer to Mary's age," he muttered.

"Twenty-two," she repeated. "A woman of that age is auld enough to ken her own mind, aye?" Old enough for marriage and bairns, certainly, although that wasn't what she was asking from him.

"Auld enough to ken what *she* wants might no' be what is best for her clan."

She frowned. Was it? By laying with Merrick—which is what *she* wanted—she might lessen her father's chance of making a marriage alliance with another clan. But there was no reason for her father to learn of this dalliance, was there?

So, she lifted her chin and boldly stared at this devil of

hers. "I'm auld enough to ken what is best for me, and ken how to get it without mucking up clan politics, *Grandda.*"

And, saints be praised! The man actually smiled at her insult. "No' yet, wee Saf. Unless Mary or Willie does something stupid, I'm a long way from being a grandda!" He poked her in the shoulder, and it felt almost *playful.* "I'm no' even twice yer age, ye ken, and I'm no' walking with a cane yet."

With the way the afternoon sun glinted off his wide shoulders, and the weight of his sword in her arms, Saffy knew he wasn't anywhere close to decrepit, so she smiled right back.

And that might've been the end of it—since she'd banished his sour mood—except Andrew and Mary chose that moment to emerge from the stables, their arms around one another, laughing.

There was hay in Mary's hair, and a love-bite on Andrew's neck.

Merrick must've realized it the same moment Saffy did, because he let out a roar, dropped the waterskin, and snatched his sword out of her hands. As Andrew instinctively pushed Mary behind him, Merrick started across the courtyard.

"Ye think to protect her from *me?*" Merrick growled, reaching the couple as Saffy ran after him. "Ye're the one who'll answer for yer sins!"

"Nay, Da—" Mary began, but Andrew interrupted her.

"I've no' sullied her, Laird."

But Merrick was drawing his sword. "*Being* with her is sullying her! I trusted ye to—"

Was the man really going to cut Andrew down? Here in front of the gathering clan members? Mary looked torn between hysterics and anger, and Saffy knew she had to do something.

"Merrick," she said softly. "Look at yer daughter."

Maybe it was the fact she'd used his name, a first in public. Andrew glanced at her in surprise, but she kept her attention on Merrick. He jerked back, as if irritated by her interruption, and when he glared at her, she kept her expression as neutral as possible, willing him to understand her point.

Saffy was someone's daughter. She knew how it felt to have her life planned out for her, whether she willed it or not.

He was the Sutherland Devil, feared and admired for his swift justice. Heaven knew she was fascinated by his quick decisions and intellect. But there were times when he needed to stop and consider another's point of view before he meted out that justice.

Finally, Merrick swung his gaze to Mary, and spent far too many heartbeats staring at his daughter. Was he remembering how it felt to save her from Robbie? Was he wondering about guilt and anger and heartbreak? It was impossible to guess.

Merrick slowly lowered the sword, and Saffy *knew* she wasn't the only one to breathe a sigh of relief. Andrew, for his part, kept his arms spread wide to prevent Mary from rushing around him. But she pushed against him, her pale eyes locked with her father's, half-pleading, half-defiant.

It was a long moment before Merrick spoke. "Mary?" he asked, his tone deadly.

"No matter how much I begged, Da, Andrew wouldnae go too far."

She said it proudly, her chin up as tears ran down her cheeks. Around them, murmurs started, and Saffy could tell from Merrick's wince that he understood what his daughter had done. Mary had taken the entire blame for the situation on her shoulders.

"And ye, lad?" Merrick said in that same low tone.

Andrew swallowed, meeting his laird's gaze bravely. "I ken she deserves better than me—"

"'Tis true," Merrick interrupted, scowling once more at his daughter. "Ye *do* deserve better than him."

Mary smiled softly. "And I love ye for thinking so, Da, but I need you to see him the way I see him. He's a good man, one *ye* taught to be good."

No one moved for several long moments. Then, to Saffy's surprise, Merrick flicked a glance her way and cocked a brow.

Was he asking for *her* opinion?

Saffy mirrored his expression, hoping he'd clarify.

He didn't. Both of his brows lowered into a scowl, and his irritation at her not answering was obvious.

She swallowed down her grin, knowing that, despite how happy the realization she could understand him without words made her, this wasn't the time for levity.

She sighed instead. "Devil, the lad is stubborn and needs more training, but"—she hurried to clarify as more than a few bystanders sucked in shocked breaths—"I *ken* ye dinnae have a more loyal or more ardent warrior than Andrew."

Merrick was holding his sword in one hand and lowered it until the tip was pointed at the ground. He stared at her with those eyes as if he couldn't understand her.

Saffy nodded, hoping she was making sense. "He's a good man, Devil. Or, he will be, assuming ye let him live. Mary loves him, and she's auld enough to ken her own mind." Would he remember their earlier conversation? "And she's strong enough to make sure he'll never dishonor her or the clan."

From the corner of her eye, she saw Mary straighten proudly, but Saffy didn't nod encouragement the way she wanted. Aye, her words were about Mary, but they were about herself, as well.

"She's strong, Devil," she whispered, "because she's yours."

Quicker than she could blink, Merrick reached out, fisting his fingers in the front of her surcoat. She barely had time to let out a surprised *"eep!"* before he yanked her toward him, until she half-dangled, nose to nose with him.

And there, in front of his daughter and Andrew, in front of his gathered clan, he kissed her.

Saffy kissed him right back.

She wrapped her arms around his neck for support, which allowed him to drop his hold on her and snake his arm around her back, pulling her closer. His lips crushed against hers, not the gentle nibbling and suckling he'd shown her beside the stream, but something passionate and primitive and glorious.

And she met him head-on, giving as good as she took.

It was long moments before the cheers penetrated her focus. She and Merrick pulled apart at the same time, and as he let her slide toward the ground, he seemed much more relaxed.

He stared down at her for a long moment, then shook his head, and looked around at his clapping and cheering clan members. "Well, lass," he said loudly, "looks like I wasn't the only one who saw through your disguise."

Saf was too shocked to make sense of his words. He'd *kissed* her. In front of everyone. When she'd been dressed as a lad! But they were all cheering—did they *all* know she hadn't been what she appeared? Andrew looked surprised, but Mary was grinning broadly and clapping enthusiastically.

Well, even if they hadn't known she was a lass, Merrick's words confirmed it.

It also meant he was no longer keeping her secret.

She should've been upset by that realization, but instead, she felt *free*. She socked him playfully in the stomach, and to her surprise, he grinned.

"Ye're the worst squire I've ever had, Saf," he said as he wrapped his arm around her shoulders and pulled her up beside him.

"Nay, I'm the only one who will challenge ye at chess," she corrected cheekily. "Although ye dinnae let me wash yer back *nearly* often enough."

He'd never actually allowed her to do that, but that didn't stop the hoots from the listeners.

Merrick rolled his eyes and steered them both toward the stables, pushing past Andrew and Mary.

"Ye are bold to speak up in the lad's defense."

"'Twas the truth I spoke."

He was silent as he released her and they stepped into the shadows of the building. "Mayhap," he finally said, heading toward his horse, "Andrew *is* a good lad."

"And Mary is a strong woman, auld enough to ken her own mind."

He paused in the action of strapping his sword to his waist and met her eyes. "The same as ye, Saf?"

"Aye."

"Will ye tell me yer real name?"

Sapphire was no saint's name. It was unique in the Highlands, mayhap in the world. If she gave it, he'd know her.

But something had changed in him when he'd kissed her that way. She couldn't keep pushing him away, not if she wanted a chance to pull him closer. To kiss him again. To see if he'd bring her as much pleasure as she was hoping.

So she finally said, "My sisters, my family...they all call me Saffy."

It wasn't the full truth, but it was enough. He jerked his chin once, and finished lashing the leather scabbard in place. Then he swung up on his horse and dug in his heels.

"Well, Saffy. Will ye help me wash my back?"

When he held his hand down to her, she knew she'd never get a better chance than this. She reached up, grasped his forearm as she placed her foot on his booted toe, and allowed him to hoist her into the saddle ahead of him.

And when they burst out of the stable, and his clan broke into cheers again, she was smiling.

CHAPTER 10

He didn't need any more bastards, but Clan Sutherland needed an heir. An undisputed son of his and his wife. It was why he'd married Elizabeth and Katharine, despite having young Willie in his heart already.

Aye, he needed an heir, and he'd have to marry to get one. In the meantime, though, he had a willing woman sitting on his lap, begging him to pleasure her.

Seeing Saf—Saffy, whoever she was—stand up to him—to *him*!—in front of his clan…

It had made Merrick see her in a new light.

She wasn't just some lass disguised as his squire. She was brilliant and passionate and witty as hell. She teased him a way no other woman had, not even Anna. Saffy met his irritation head-on, and had the guts to stay his hand when he was prepared to mete out justice.

She'd saved Andrew yet again, hadn't she?

He was done fighting himself. She was unlike any other woman he'd known, and he wanted to taste her, to make her scream his name. He could do that without planting his babe in her belly.

He wasn't sure who she was, but he was done fighting this attraction to her.

Smiling, he lowered his chin and nuzzled against the side of her neck. He liked the way she sighed and tilted her head to give him better access. As his lips skimmed over her skin, he couldn't decide if he appreciated her short hair or not. It meant less hair in his way, but he couldn't sweep it out of the way. What would she look like wet?

The thought of Saf naked and dripping wet made him hungry.

"Where are ye taking me?" she murmured.

Anywhere ye want. But instead he said, "Somewhere close. Where we can be alone, and ye can finally wash my back, as ye've been begging."

"Good," she said. "Ye stink like a man who's been training all day."

He dragged his tongue across the smooth skin below her ear, reveling in her delicate taste and loving the way she shivered.

"Ye like it," he growled.

"Aye."

When she shifted in his lap, his cock jumped in excitement, and he found himself grinning against her skin. It was like the decision he'd made had lifted a weight from his shoulders.

He nudged the horse to move faster.

"Is it safe?" she asked suddenly.

Knowing she was thinking of the attack from the Lindsays, he grunted. "'Tisnae far from the keep, but nae one will bother us." He tightened his hold around her middle, hating the thought of her fear. "I'll no' let harm come to ye again, ye have my word."

"I trust ye."

He used his chin to move some of her hair to one side. "Aye, *Saffy*? Enough to tell me why ye're on my land?"

It was like she knew he was trying to keep the mood light. "Nay, Devil, no' quite that much."

Despite her denial, her tone was light, and he found himself chuckling.

They reached the waterfall soon enough, and he swung down and reached for her. "With the horse here to announce our presence, we'll no' be disturbed."

She was looking around in wonder. "So, we'll be completely alone? To do whatever we wish?"

No' quite whatever *ye wish, lass.*

He shrugged and moved toward the bank. To his left, the stream tumbled from a height twice a man's reach, over a series of boulders until dropping off and crashing into the pool before him. He knew from past explorations that the area behind the last fall was private, and a bit magical.

Were he the sort of man to believe in magic, that is.

He felt her move beside him, and when she slipped her little hand into his, he turned and smiled down at her.

"'Tis beautiful here," she whispered, staring at the waterfall, its roar nigh covering her words.

"Aye." As he agreed, he pulled her away from the water, away from the noise. "I thought ye might like it here. We have much to discuss." Like his announcement that he had every intention of giving in to her seduction, if not actually claiming her as his own.

She hummed, but followed willingly. "Like what? Ye didnae drag me out here to punish my boldness?"

With a small grin, he wrapped his arms around her, and liked the way she laced her fingers behind his waist and cocked her head back to meet his eyes.

"Yer boldness deserves *some* sort of response, 'tis true. What do ye suggest?"

"Hm. Well," she said with a shrug, "I suppose I could take all my clothes off and climb over yer lap, and ye could punish my bare arse."

His brows rose. "And that's something ye think ye would enjoy?"

"Oh, nay." Her eyes twinkled as she wriggled against him. "I was rather counting on ye being distracted once ye had me in yer lap."

He had to chuckle at that. "I would be, aye. And I have nae intention of punishing ye." He blew out a breath. "Nae one, not even Gavin, has had the audacity to stay my hand when I was prepared to mete out justice."

"Nae one?" Her brows rose in surprise.

Well, there'd been once... "Many years ago, I caught a lad reiving on my lands. He was part of an outlaw band, but I caught him with the ewe in his arms, so I hanged him." He watched her pale slightly, and wondered at it. "He didnae die instantly, but I was determined to mete out justice. I should've drawn my sword and ended it. When the laird I was with finally drew his dirk, I assumed that was his plan, but he cut down the lad and lectured me on second chances."

"And the lad?" she asked with a strangled whisper. "What of him?"

"He devoted himself to that laird." The name of the Sinclair Hound, the loyal bodyguard, was whispered in awe throughout the Highlands. "And despite my anger at the man countering my justice, I saw the rightness in letting the lad live. 'Tis why I..."

He shook his head, not needing to go into the story of his attempted alliance with the Sinclairs. But she pushed.

"Why, what?"

Speaking of his past, of hard lessons learned, had softened his ardor somewhat. He loosened his hold on her and sunk down on a thick patch of grass. Still holding his hand, she followed.

"'Tis why, in the spring, I approached that laird and requested a marriage alliance with one of his daughters. Allying with the Sinclairs would allow us to stand strong against the Mackenzies. Not only because of our matching strength, but because one of Sinclair's other daughters is now married to the Mackenzie Regent."

She dropped his hand and pulled her knees up to her chin, then wrapped her arms around them. He knew he hadn't confused her—not with her sharp mind—so what was she thinking to make her frown like that?

"Is that the only reason you made the alliance?"

The alliance had fallen apart when the daughter Duncan Sinclair had offered broke the contract to take holy vows. Only, Merrick had heard she'd married someone else instead. No need to bother Saf with all that.

He shrugged, resting his elbow on one knee and staring at the waterfall.

"I needed an heir. I still do, I suppose. Willie is a good lad, smart and strong. But his mother..."

"Anna," she said in a strange voice.

He glanced at her and frowned at the way she was hugging herself. "Aye," he muttered, shifting until he was close enough to touch her. He rested his weight on the hand he planted in the grass behind her back. "Anna was...I was barely a man when I met her. She was aulder than me, but had a love for life that made me...*happy*."

Whatever he'd said must've touched something in her, because Saf's shoulders loosened with a sigh, and she dropped her arms from her knees. "Will ye tell me about her?"

He shrugged again. "No' much to tell. Da refused to let me marry her, but that wasnae unusual. He had a dozen bastard children, of course, and so did his father. The whispers say that when a Sutherland laird joins with a lass, she'll bear his babe." It shouldn't be possible, but it was hard to ignore the evidence. "I thought I'd follow in his footsteps, until…" Until he'd held wee Mary, then wee Willie, and known he'd move heaven and hell for them. "Well, once I became laird, maybe I would've married her. But Anna died bringing another bairn into the world."

Her hand covered his. "I'm sorry, Merrick. Did ye love her?"

He blew out a breath. "Aye," he said simply. "Da told me I was a fool, but I'm no' sure the man kenned how to love."

"'Tis so hard to lose someone we love."

Her fingers threaded through his, and they sat like that for a few minutes, watching the waterfall. He wasn't sure what she was thinking of, but he wasn't thinking of Anna, not anymore. She held a place in his heart, and he'd always be grateful for his time with her, and the gifts of their children together.

But the woman sitting beside him…*Saf* was the one who held his attention now.

Held his heart?

A smile tugged at his lips. The Sutherland Devil falling for a lass's spell? What would his men say?

And did he care?

"And yer wives?"

Her quiet question jerked him out of his musings, and he glanced at her. "What about them?"

"Did ye love them as well?"

Had he really never spoken of Elizabeth and Katharine to her? He shrugged and lay back on the ground, his fingers still twined with hers, and his other arm stacked behind his head. It was easier to speak of them than Anna.

"Da made the alliance with Elizabeth's father to strengthen our southern border. But when she arrived for the wedding, she was nothing like we expected."

"Oh?" She shifted until she was sitting cross-legged beside his hip, holding his hand in both of hers.

He closed his eyes, enjoying the peace, despite the topic. "She was young, aye, and verra beautiful. But she was little more than a child, and too sickly for a braw young man."

She snorted and poked his thigh hard enough to make him growl. But when she began to rub and knead the spot she'd poked, the sound turned into a groan of satisfaction. Who knew the muscles in his thighs were that tight?

"Elizabeth?" she prompted, her hand working down to his knee.

"She…" He sighed in pleasure. "She wanted to take holy vows. But her father had threatened her, so she cried through the ceremony and confessed before I could take her to bed. She was so frail…" He shook his head, trying to banish the memory of the wee lass sobbing in fear in his bed, her skin so pale it was nearly translucent. "She was more ill than anyone kenned. I couldnae have bedded her, even if I'd had the inclination."

"What happened?"

He swallowed past the memory of those dark days. "She wasted away some months after the wedding. I sent for the abbess a sennight before, released Elizabeth from the marriage, despite Da's objections, and she was able to take vows."

He could hear the smile in Saf's voice when she spoke. "She died a nun." When she poked him in the thigh again, it didn't hurt as much. "Ye *do* have a heart, Devil!"

Remembering the way Elizabeth's small hand had felt in his as he'd sat by her bed, he winced. "I hated watching her, kenning how easy it was to catch ill and slip away. I spent most of my days training, trying to forget that…but Da made another contract before Elizabeth was cold in the ground."

"I'm sorry."

"I didnae think much of it. 'Twas the way of things, I suppose. Katharine was lusty enough, I suppose, but I'd learned my lesson with Anna and Elizabeth, and refused to let her into my heart."

Saf hummed. "Maggie is about the age to have come from that union?"

That wasn't a topic he was prepared to discuss, so he pulled his leg from under her hands and sat up once more, the abrupt motion startling her into leaning back.

"I told ye Sutherland men have nae problem planting babes. Katharine fell pregnant on our wedding night, and died —the bairn with her—from a fall on the ice on the keep's steps six months later."

The beautiful, bold woman next to him gasped, her eyes wide with pity. "Oh, Merrick," she finally whispered. "I'm so sorry."

His chin jerked once in acknowledgement as he ran his suddenly sweaty palms down his kilted thighs.

Why was his heart pounding? Because of how close she'd come to his secret? Or because despite that fact, despite talking of poor Elizabeth and Katharine, his cock was still hard, just because of her touch?

He swallowed. "They deserved better, but I tried to give them both what they wanted. They were good lasses—good *women*—and they kenned their own minds."

With one fluid movement, Saf pushed herself to her feet and kicked off her shoes. Then she shrugged off her surcoat.

"What are ye doing?" he asked in a hoarse voice.

"Undressing." She pulled her shirt from over her head and used the bottom of one foot to roll down the opposite stocking, then the other. Her breeches followed. In a matter of moments, she stood clad in only her braies and the linen wrapping around her breasts.

When had he stood up? He couldn't recall. All he knew was

that she held him in some sort of spell, and his pulse was pounding in his temple. "Saf?" he choked out.

"Anna and Elizabeth and Katharine kenned their own minds, Merrick," she said, her hands on her hips and her tone scolding him. "Ye saw it with them, and respected them for it. And just an hour ago, I saw ye reconsider yer intentions and acknowledge that yer own daughter is a strong woman whose opinion should be respected."

Mary? How did Mary come into this?

Merrick shook his head, trying to clear his thoughts...but they kept coming back to how *lickable* she looked standing there in the dappled shade beside the pool.

Unfortunately, she took that as denial. "*Aye,*" she said firmly. "Ye are a good man, Devil, despite the stories. All I ask now is that ye trust me when I say I ken my own mind, my own desires."

With that, she reached for the knot under her left arm and set to work untying the linen strip around her chest. As she unwound it, she held his eyes in challenge.

But when the linen at last pooled around her feet, Merrick's gaze dropped.

Gods wounds, but she had beautiful breasts. Small and perky and just right for his hands.

He fisted his hands at his sides, his palms itching from the memory of the way he'd cupped them last night in the darkness. But to see them like this, free and proud in the sunlight...? His mouth went dry.

She dropped her hand to the waist of her braies. "Ye're overdressed, Merrick, if ye want me to scrub yer back."

As soon as her braies hit the grass at her feet, she turned and jumped into the pool.

He was still rocked by that glimpse of the curls between her legs and the flash of her bare arse. But the shocked noise she made as she hit the cold water had him grinning.

Somehow his clothing joined hers on the grass.

They came together in the center of the pool, where the water was deepest. He could stand, the water lapping against his chest. It seemed natural for her to wrap her arms around him and allow him to support her.

The way her breasts rubbed against his bare chest, the water lapping both of them, had his cock jumping against her belly, and she smiled.

"I didnae drag ye out here to wash my back, Saf," he warned in a low tone.

"Aye?" She wiggled against him, causing him to suck in a breath between his teeth. "Then why am I here?"

"What ye did today, what ye said…" God's wounds, but it was hard to concentrate with her in his arms, all slippery and willing. "Ye *are* a strong woman, Saf. And I respect ye enough to believe ye ken what ye want. And ye've made what ye want verra clear."

"I want ye, Merrick."

"I love the way ye say my name," he admitted.

"Which is why I so rarely use it, Devil," she teased.

"Aye?" he growled as he lowered his mouth to the skin at the base of her neck. "Ye confess?"

"*Aye*, Merrick!" she cried as she wrapped her legs around his waist. "I want ye."

His lips trailed over her shoulder.

With her hanging on like this, his cock was so close to her warmth, he could barely stand it. When she moaned and shifted impatiently, his thick staff slid between them in a delicious mockery of what he *wanted* to be doing.

But his long-ago vow limited him to just pleasuring *her*, and that's what he'd focus on.

Of course, the damn vow was hard to remember when he lifted her to draw one perfect, pert nipple into his mouth, and she made the most erotic sound he'd ever heard.

"Merrick!" Her fingers wrapped in his hair as her head dropped back. "*Please!*"

This wasn't the place for it. But there was *a* place he wanted to share with her.

He straightened and pulled her closer as he pushed his way toward the waterfall. She met his gaze just as they reached it.

She was the woman for him. She matched him completely.

Smiling, he tightened his hold on her and plunged through the wall of water.

Behind it, there was a small rock ledge where he and Gavin and Robbie and the other lads used to play at as children. The bottom sloped up, until the water was barely knee-deep.

He carried her to the ledge and placed her bare arse on the carpet of moss which grew there. He'd made the right choice to share this place with her. The power of the water was clear and never failed to make his heart pound.

But when she smiled in excitement, his heart pounded for an entirely different reason. And when she opened her arms and beckoned him to return, he almost lost his resolve and plunged into her right then and there.

But her joy, her determination, was why they were there.

So he showed her what she meant to him with his mouth, hands, and fingers.

When he circled her nipple with his tongue, then nipped at it, she gasped, then groaned. He used that chance to drop one hand to her curls, stroking his thumb through her slit.

"Merrick," she sighed in pleasure and dropped her weight back on one splayed palm. The other hand rose to the back of his head, as if to hold him in place.

Aye, she was a lass who knew what she wanted!

He switched his attention to the other nipple, his hand replacing his mouth on the first one as she squirmed under his touch. Between one heartbeat and the next, he slipped a finger inside her.

She relaxed against him and pressed her hips upward in a silent plea. His thumb circled her pearl as he slipped another finger inside her, and she arched against him.

"Merrick!"

Aye, that was all the urging he needed. God in Heaven, but he wanted nothing more than to slam his cock home.

He wouldn't.

Instead, he dropped to his knees, his hips just above the cold water, and lowered his mouth to her opening.

The noise she made was somewhere between a sob and a moan as he dragged his tongue along her slit, then circling her pearl. He used his thumb to press against her, to coax her into release.

Under his assault, she moaned and squirmed and called his name in a way which made him proud. He was giving her what she wanted, aye?

The familiar pressure built behind his ballocks, and he wished he could do more than lick her. Her muscles tightened around him, and he knew she was close.

Suddenly, she clamped her thighs tight. "Devil take you, Merrick!" she panted. "This isnae—"

When she cut herself off with a groan, Merrick pulled himself to his feet. Her tongue darted across her lips as she stared at him, standing before her.

"Lass?" he growled.

"I want…" She arched against his touch, then met his eyes. "I want *ye*, Merrick!"

"Aye, lass," he said gently, not even sure she could hear him over the water.

Still holding her gaze, he pushed his fingers into her once more, and he saw the frustration in her eyes as she began to shake her head. But her eyes flew open once more as he felt her inner muscles tighten around him, and her head lolled back as she found her release with a sigh.

His fingers continued to stroke her gently as he watched her relax on the ledge.

Finally, her eyes opened, and she frowned at him.

"Why?" she demanded.

It was hard to hear over the rushing water, so he shook his head. "I'll no' risk getting ye with child, Saf."

"What?"

He knew he wasn't going to find release now—possibly ever again, now that he'd given her what she wanted—so he scooped her up in his arms and pushed them back through the waterfall.

She buried her face against his shoulder and endured the cold.

They sloshed through the pool toward the grassy bank, where he gently laid her down and hoisted himself up as well. Once there, he couldn't resist pulling her into his arms, his cock still pressed between them.

"Ye ken the Sutherland reputation, lass," he explained gently, hoping to ease her irritation. "Watching ye stand up to me today in defense of Andrew, made me see how strong ye are. Ye ken what's best for the clan, and that's a rare talent. Ye dinnae deserve to bear my bastard."

"Did Anna?"

He couldn't tell what she was thinking. She was watching him carefully, the light of *something* in those dark blue eyes, and he winced at the question.

"I was younger then and didnae understand what it meant. But ye—ye could be anyone. And since ye refuse to trust me with yer name, I'll no' risk—"

She interrupted him by reaching up and grasping his cheeks and pulling him down for a kiss.

It was a kiss filled with promise and apology and understanding and so much more.

She was the one who pushed him away, his face still in her hands.

"Ye'll no' risk a bastard, but if ye kenned my family, what would ye do?"

"I'd…" He shook his head, his mind still muddled. "I dinnae ken." He needed an heir, aye, but there was no telling if her clan would be willing to align with him.

Her nose was mere inches from his, his arms pressed between her slick back and the thick grass, and when she grinned, he sucked in a breath.

"Sapphire," she said suddenly.

He blinked. "What?"

"My name is Sapphire. I'm one of the Sinclair Jewels."

CHAPTER 11

Saffy held her breath, staring into his eyes and praying she'd made the right decision.

He blinked and shook his head slightly, as if disbelieving. She tightened her hold on his face and nodded, willing him to understand what she was saying.

He exhaled softly. "Sapphire."

"Sinclair."

"So Pearl is…"

"My youngest sister, aye." Pinned beneath him, still somehow unfulfilled despite her earlier release, Saffy wriggled her hips. "She was worthy enough for you, Merrick. Am I?"

He reared back as if he'd been hit, and she let him go, her hands falling to his shoulders, praying he wasn't leaving her.

"Sapphire," he croaked again, then closed his eyes tightly.

Between them, she felt his member jump, and longed to reach down to touch him the way he'd touched himself. Slowly, she began to inch her legs apart, hoping he'd take the hint.

"Devil," she whispered, "Ye were willing to align with my father once afore, and I am my father's daughter."

Mayhap it was her words, or mayhap her actions, or mayhap he was contemplating something totally different. Whatever it was, she saw the moment he quit fighting, the moment he gave into her pleas.

With a groan, he dropped his mouth to hers, then lightly kissed her cheek and jaw and neck. Triumphantly, she spread her legs, her core already aching with need once more, and didn't bother to hold back the breathy chuckle which escaped her in anticipation.

"Lass," he growled, pushing himself up on one arm and reaching between them with the other to grasp his erection. "Ye're the worthiest woman I ken. Are ye sure this is what ye want?"

She held his gaze, despite the way her blood thrummed, urging her to arch against him, to grab him, to make him *hers*.

"Ye're what I want."

"God's wounds, Saf," he whispered, closing his eyes on a shudder.

She tightened her hold on his shoulders, trying to pull him closer, but only succeeding in lifting herself off the grass. "*Now*, please," she commanded.

His lips twitched, and he opened his eyes once more. "Aye, lass."

Her core was still wet from her release—or mayhap it was in readiness for his entry. Without dropping her gaze, he stroked her once, twice, and she bucked against him. Her mouth opened on another plea, and he grinned.

He positioned himself between her legs, then halted at her entrance. She groaned in frustration and tried to press lower, to impale herself.

"Saf?" he asked again, his voice hoarse.

"Aye! Aye, Merrick, hurry—*Merrick!*" she cried as he moved, then froze.

The pain of being *stretched* caused Saffy's eyes to fly open, her breaths coming too fast. But she focused on his lips, which were pressed in a hard line, then rose to his eyes. The expression in them was unreadable, the lines at their corners showed his concern.

He was holding himself back. *For her.* That, as much as his concern, eased the pain. Or mayhap it was the time which passed. Saf took a deep breath, then another…and miraculously, the feeling of *stretching* was replaced by a different feeling.

She wasn't just being stretched, but *filled.*

He was filling her the way she'd imagined, the way she'd hoped. The way she and her sisters giggled about. The way a man, his velvet-encased steel aching with need, took a woman he cared for.

That realization, more than anything, made her smile. The sensation of being filled—by her Devil!—caused a flood of warmth to spiral through her limbs. She shifted under him, pulling her legs up, and planting her bare feet on the ground by his thighs, bracketing his hips with her knees.

The motion helped sink him even deeper into her, and she caught her breath.

"Saf?" he asked again.

Under him, she moved—just slightly. A simple back and forth, a tiny movement. But both of them sucked in a gasp.

"Please, Merrick," she moaned. "Dinnae make me do this all myself."

He didn't.

If his first thrust made her gasp, then the second felt as if it sucked all the air out of her body, and by the third…well, she held on to his shoulders and lifted her rear end off the ground and met him thrust for thrust, until she felt as if she could leave her own body and float above the earth on a cloud of pleasure and joy.

The pressure built between her legs, just above where his

member claimed her. As the ache began to border on frustrating, he dropped one hand between them and pressed his thumb against the center of her pleasure.

She jerked upright, plastering herself against his chest and screaming his name as *something* crashed over her. White lights exploded behind her eyes, and she clamped her knees around him in an effort to understand this breathless wonder.

With her holding on, he thrust twice more, threw his head back, and *roared*.

A warm flood of *him* spread throughout her body, and she knew this was what she'd been waiting for.

If she'd had breath left, she would've yelled her joy right along with him.

With a groan, he lowered himself to the grass beside her, slipping from her. Part of her mourned the lost connection, but another was too busy gasping in joy.

Now I ken why Pearl's always smiling.

The thought bubbled up inside her like laughter, and she had to open her mouth to let it escape, lest she burst with contentment.

"That was incredible!"

She rolled to her side, intent on thanking him. But he wasn't looking at her. Merrick lay on his back, his member already softening against his belly, his chest heaving, and his eyes wide as he stared up at the leafy canopy.

"Devil?" she prompted, propping herself up on one elbow and throwing a leg over his. "Are ye aright?"

His breathing slowed, but nothing else moved. At long last, he turned to meet her eyes.

"'Twas everything I needed, Saf." He winced and shook his head. "I broke my vow," he whispered as he closed his eyes.

Unable to stop the jolt of worry which coursed through her, she placed her hand on his chest. "What do ye mean?"

"Nae more bastards."

That was all he said. All he had to say.

Saf let out a breath and withdrew her hand, to rest it over her stomach. As her eyes widened, she exhaled softly. Could she already be pregnant? He'd said that Sutherland men were unusually potent, but was it the right time of the month for her? She tried to count the days in her head, but her thoughts were too jumbled to concentrate.

Nae more bastards.

That had been his vow. That was why he'd rejected her offers; however subtle they'd been. That was why he hadn't planned on joining with her.

But he had, and it had been as glorious as she'd hoped. And if the rumors were right, she could even now be carrying his child. Interestingly, the thought of bearing his babe, even if it meant having to find her own way in the world, wasn't as horrible as she might have thought. Mayhap it was the feeling of *rightness* following her release, but at that moment, the only thing she was praying for was that the babe would have his father's dark hair and unusual eyes, unlike most of Merrick's children.

After Emma's birth, only a few months ago, he must've decided to stop his carousing.

"Yer vow didnae last long, Devil," she said with a teasing grin, dragging her fingers across her own stomach, loving how *alive* her skin felt.

Had she ever been completely nude in nature this way? Well, certainly not *this* way! A chuckle escaped her.

At the sound, he scowled and rolled to face her with a quickness which startled her.

"Twelve years, *Saf*," he growled, his pale eyes full of something she couldn't identify.

Shame?

He didn't give her time to consider it. "I'd promised myself long ago I'd not join with another woman. I'd not risk siring more bastards."

"But wee Emma—" she began in confusion, but he interrupted.

"And I've held to that vow." He planted one elbow and loomed over her, grabbing her hip with his free hand and pulling her flush against him. "But *ye*, Sapphire Sinclair, I broke that vow for *ye*."

Her heart had begun to pound, both at his nearness and his intensity.

Blessed Virgin, but he was being dramatic, wasn't he?

She lifted her chin and met his glare. "And I'll thank the saints every day ye did, Devil."

He began to roll his eyes at *her* dramatic claim, but she stopped him with a poke in the chest. "I'll thank the saints ye considered me at least as worthy of vow-breaking as you did the others."

He frowned. "Others?"

He wasn't that dense, was he? "Your other *lovers*. The ones in whose bellies you planted your babes."

With a noise which might've been a laugh, and might've been a groan, he fell back to the grass once more. Since he hadn't released her, she went with him, toppling across him and not minding it at all.

"Merrick, ye didnae think me even as worthy as—"

"They're no' mine."

Her lips snapped shut as she stared down at him in shock. His gaze drifted from her to the leaves beyond her head.

"They're no' mine," he repeated, softer. "They're the children of my heart, but no' of my body. Anna bore Mary and Willie."

His skin was warm against hers, but she was too shocked to enjoy the sensation. "The rest...?"

"I sired none of them, no' even wee Beck, who more than a

few people have said is my punishment for my own rambunctious childhood." His breath escaped on a chuckle, and he lifted his head to meet her eyes. "They're likely all Sutherlands, aye, sired by uncles or brothers I never even kenned. Maggie is one of Robbie's gets, and possibly Nolan as well."

She shook her head, still trying to wrap her mind around the news. The Sutherland Devil's band of bastards weren't his own?

"Have ye ever asked?" she began hesitantly.

"Asked their mothers?" He shook his head. "Nay. By turning their children over to me, they ken the bairns will be raised healthy and happy, with as much status as I can grant them. It's in the bairns' best interests for the world to consider them mine, so I never dispute their mothers' lies."

He was right. She knew it with a certainty she hadn't expected. The children he was raising, the bairns the world assumed were his...their lives were so much better as beloved children of a powerful laird. Had Merrick denied them, had he exposed their mothers' lies, and sent them away, they would not have the access to the education, training, and healthy living he provided.

And as he said, they *were* Sutherlands.

But with his vow, he'd made sure that the next generation wouldn't have his same worries. There'd be no Robbies, no John Lindsays, intent on making life difficult for the Sutherlands. And once he sired a legitimate heir...

"And if you marry again?" she managed to choke past the lump in her throat.

He held her gaze. "I cannae promise there will be nae more. As long as a bairn needs a home..."

She nodded, understanding.

"They are..." She cleared her throat, cursing the tears in her eyes. "They are Sutherlands, after all."

His arms found their way to her backside, and he pressed

her against him. Saffy expected the movement to stir passion in both of them, but instead, she felt a fierce sort of contentment, a *fullness* rising in her chest.

"Ye understand me, lass? Ye understand why I fought yer charms for so long?"

"Aye, and I love ye for it."

His dark brows shot up. "Ye do?"

"Aye!" At his expression, she began to laugh, despite the tears which threatened. "Aye! I love ye, Merrick Sinclair, and I'll thank every saint which led me to yer keep."

"*Every* saint?"

"Well," she clarified, chuckling, "I could've done without the stay in yer dungeon, so mayhap no' St. Andrew."

Slowly, a grin pulled his lips wide. "And since ye ken my secret now, lass, and since ye've declared me worthy of *ye*, mayhap ye could explain what a Sinclair Jewel is doing sneaking into my keep in the first place?"

Could she? She'd kept so many secrets—her sex, her identity, her mission—for so long, it was hard to remember her reasons.

"Saf?" He prompted. "Do ye no' trust me?"

Slowly, her smile bloomed. She *did.* "I do," she admitted.

"Then ye'll tell me?"

There, lying beside the pool, cushioned by his body, and blanketed by his arms, she explained the mystery of the missing jewels. She told him about Pearl's find of the ancient tapestry, which led Agata to the Mackenzie holding. She told him how Agata had found one of the jewels hidden under the Sutherland holding on an ancestral wooden map.

Merrick seemed close to laughter. "And so ye came to my land, to what? To find a connection between my clan and yers? Do ye think my ancestor stole yer jewels?"

She blew out an exasperated breath and dug her elbows into his chest, ignoring his wince to prop her chin on her palms. "Nay, any more than I think the Mackenzies stole them. But…"

"But?"

"*But* yer grandfather and my great grandfather married sisters. They were originally from the Campbell clan."

"Aye, we've had an alliance with them going back that long."

"The jewels disappeared right around the time one of the sisters came to marry my great grandda—she was his second wife. One of her sisters went to the Mackenzies, and one to the Sutherlands."

Gently, he coaxed her elbows out of the way, until she collapsed against him. His expression was thoughtful.

"That *is* more compelling, I'll admit."

Excited he was considering her theory, she straightened once more. "So, have ye seen anything which might mean the jewels are here? I've combed the tapestries and the histories, but I found naught—" She broke off when he began to chuckle. "What?"

"Nay, I've heard naught. I'll help ye search, but I'm remembering how Andrew reported he'd discovered ye 'sneaking about' and ye claimed an interest in tapestries."

Her lips twitched. "See? I told ye the lad was loyal."

He sobered instantly. "Ye did, and likely saved his hide. I intended to punish him for sullying Mary."

"She claimed he didnae, and I believe her. Do ye?"

His arm snaked around her once more. "I do. But I wouldnae have taken the time to listen to her claims, had ye no' forced me to."

"We make a good team, then. Ye act swiftly, precisely, and I'll point out when ye're being an idiot."

When his laughter rumbled through his chest, she felt it in the very core of her being.

Finally, he rested his head against the grass, his eyes closed, and a smile on his lips. She decided this was the most handsome she'd ever seen him. The dappled sunlight made the silver at his temples sparkle, and the lines around his eyes were softer than she'd ever seen.

I did that.

Pride and contentment rose up in her as she laid in his arms and drew small circles on his chest.

"Ye're right," he murmured. "We *do* make a good team. Seeing ye stand up to me today, seeing ye speak for the good of the clan…that's when I quit fighting it, Saf." His eyes were still closed. "Ye might make a terrible squire, but ye're a damn fine chess partner."

"And lover?" she prompted, surprised she wasn't shy about the question. She *knew* he'd enjoyed himself as much as she had.

"Aye," he drawled, his hands cupping her arse. "The best I've had in years."

"I'm the *only* lover ye've—"

She cut off the indignant rebuttal with a gasp as he rolled with lightning speed, flipping her over on her back until *he* was the one grinning above her.

"Aye, a fine lover, indeed, Saf." He brushed a kiss against her lips, but before she could deepen it, pulled back. "And seeing yer boldness, yer intelligence, and yer wise counsel today…I realized ye'd make a fine Lady Sutherland, as well."

She only had time to suck in a shocked breath before he continued.

"I didnae ken yer family name or why ye were in my home. But I kenned enough about ye to understand *that*, at least. I couldnae marry ye, no' without kenning the rest, but…"

But now that he *did* know? "But?" she prompted.

He kissed her again, as gently as a butterfly brushing against her skin. When he pulled back, his expression was…nervous?

"I made a contract once already with yer father, Saf. The alliance would be good for both of us, and he's proven amenable to having me as a son-in-law."

She stopped breathing.

"Aye," she croaked in agreement. Was he saying what she thought he was saying?

He held her gaze. "I want ye by my side, Saf. If I asked him, do ye think he'd agree to a marriage contract with *yer* name on it?"

She exhaled.

"Are ye sure he's the one ye want to ask that question?"

"Will ye marry me, Saf? Be my lady? Bear my heirs?"

As her heart leapt with joy, she pursed her lips and hummed.

"I dinnae ken. I'm a loyal squire, ye understand. I'll have to ask my master if he'd agree—What are ye doing?" she asked with a yelp as he rolled to his feet in one movement, tossing her over his shoulder as he did so.

He stooped to grab her clothes before heading for the well-trained horse who'd been waiting silently nearby. She gave another yelp when he bounced her once before tossing her onto the saddle and handing her the linen shirt.

She pulled it over her head and emerged to find him still grinning up at her, naked as the day he was born, his erection proudly jutting from its nest of wiry curls.

"I'm taking ye back to my chambers, squire, where ye'll learn to put that clever mouth of yers to work convincing me."

"Convincing *ye?*" she demanded indignantly, trying to figure out how to pull on her breeches while seated atop a horse. "Ye think to…" Since she couldn't figure out how to finish that thought, she didn't.

He was outright chuckling as he wrapped his kilt and belted it, then jammed on his boots, and swung up behind her.

One arm wrapped around her, resting protectively on her stomach, his fingers just brushing the underside of her breasts.

"Aye, lass," he growled in her ear, sending shivers through her. "I'll make ye *beg*."

And as he kicked his horse into motion, Saf gave up caring about her modesty. Laughing, she tossed her breeches into the blurred bushes as they rushed past, and when he joined in, she felt his joy in her very soul.

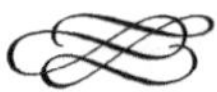

CHAPTER 12

"Laird! Merrick!"

Merrick woke slowly, which was unusual, but likely due to the woman in his arms.

How long had it been since he'd woken this way? He and Katharine had shared a bed, aye, but Anna was the last he'd held this way. And his feelings for Saf…

Well, he wasn't sure yet. He'd loved Anna, but Saf made him feel *alive* in a way he hadn't in years. And not just because she matched him in bed, but her wit, her joy, her—

"Merrick! Open up!"

Ah, that's what had woken him—the pounding on the door. Funny, it sounded like Gavin's voice, but the man was still in the healer's chamber, unable to remain awake long enough to account for his piss-poor decisions.

Slowly, Merrick moved out from under Saf. She murmured sleepily and moaned as she rolled off him.

"Who is it?" she asked hoarsely, and he smiled at how exhausted she sounded.

They'd returned from the waterfall with his kilt askew and her half-naked in his arms, but it didn't matter. He'd called for

Corra to send supper to his chambers, then marched right past his chuckling and cheering clan to carry Saf up the stairs. Even Mary stood, grinning happily, little Isobel in her arms.

Merrick had tossed Saf on his bed, where she'd rolled to her stomach. The sight of that bare arse in the air had been more than his control—finally relinquished after so many years!—could stand. He pulled her up to her knees, pressed her shoulders into the mattress, and showed her a few new positions which she—apparently—had found quite satisfactory.

Aye, it had been a long and glorious night, and who in the hell thought it was aright to wake them with the stars still high in the dark sky?

"Merrick! Please!"

The pounding was beginning to sound desperate by the time Merrick untangled himself from the coverlets and Saf.

She was sitting up in bed now, rubbing her eyes. "What's going on?"

It was *her* interrupted sleep more than his own which sent Merrick stomping nude to the door in a foul temper. He'd just begun to build a future with this woman, and now someone had the bollocks to bother them?

He yanked open the door just as another round of frantic knocking began, and was surprised to see Gavin standing there, fist raised, his other hand locked around the wrist of…

"Elana?" Merrick frowned, his gaze going back to his friend, whose expression was a mix of terror and relief.

"Merrick, thank God," Gavin muttered with relief, pushing past him to tug his younger sister into the room.

Elana was carrying a lit taper, and as she passed Merrick, he sucked in a surprised breath. The lass was wearing naught but a torn chemise and was covered in filth. Not only that, her face and arms showed bruises and cuts as if…as if a man had used his fists to beat her.

The pair halted in the middle of the room, Gavin's frantic gaze searching the corners as if for danger, not even lingering on Saf, who'd pulled the coverlet up around her shoulders.

Merrick's eyes narrowed as he slammed the door and stalked toward the man whom he'd always trusted.

"What in the hell is going on, Gavin? Why are ye no' unconscious?"

"I'm—I'm sorry." The other man shook his head, the light from his sister's candle catching the healed scar on his forehead. "I truly am, Merrick," he said hoarsely.

It was the guilt in his friend's eyes, more than anything, which made Merrick realize the truth. Gavin hadn't been in and out of consciousness for the last sennight. The reason the healer couldn't determine what was wrong with him was because there *wasn't* anything wrong.

Gavin had been pretending for days, to avoid having to answer for his failures.

With a growl, Merrick spun away from the two of them to scoop up his kilt. He recalled Saf tearing it from his body last night, but he couldn't let himself focus on that memory. Not if he wanted to get to the bottom of this midnight intrusion.

"What have ye done, Gavin?" he asked as he belted the material around his waist. "Why are ye here?"

His friend swallowed and met his eyes, nodding once. "Aye, Laird. I…" He exhaled, and tugged his sister to him.

Elana wrapped her arms around her brother and pressed her cheek to his chest. "Thank ye, Gav," she said in a choked whisper.

"Aye, lass." Gavin sounded equally sad as he pressed a kiss to the top of her head, and Merrick's stomach clenched in dread.

Gently, Gavin pulled his sister's arms from around his waist, and pushed her toward Saf, who'd wrapped the coverlet around herself and was now climbing out of the bed to light more tapers. "Go on, Elana. Remember what ye need to tell them, after 'tis done. I love ye."

"Nay, Gav!" she cried, her voice breaking on a sob. "Nay!" But she stumbled into Saf's arms.

Saf caught the poor girl and looked to Merrick for guidance, but his friend's fear had infected the laird as well.

"Gavin?" he growled.

That's when his second-in-command and the man he trusted most in the world, drew his sword and brandished it before him.

Merrick had just enough time to curse himself a fool—why in damnation had he opened the door without a weapon—when Gavin surprised him again. The man sunk to his knees in front of Merrick, holding his weapon up as an offering.

Merrick caught his breath, but before he could ask again what was going on, his friend spoke.

"Laird, I'm the traitor. I've been planting false trails for yer scouts to follow, leading them away from Lindsay's men. I led our men into that ambush."

Rage, white-hot and near-blinding, tore through Merrick.

Gavin! He trusted him and had been betrayed? And it wasn't just that his second had delayed Lindsay's reckoning, it was…

"Saf was wounded in that battle, ye son-of-a-bitch!"

Gavin said nothing, but met his gaze with a look of acceptance and sorrow.

With a roar and a burning need for swift action and decisive justice, Merrick snatched the offered sword out of his once-friend's hands. Gavin lowered his arms with a faint sigh, and bent his head forward, prepared to accept the undeserved, quick death.

Ignoring Elana's cry of "Gavin, nay!" Merrick lifted the man's own sword to deliver that swift justice.

And would've struck the blow, killing the man who'd once been his friend, had Saf not stopped him.

She appeared so suddenly, standing between him and the kneeling Gavin, that Merrick nearly wrenched his shoulder halting his swing in time.

"Devil!" she cried, one arm holding the coverlet to her, the other raised in a plea.

"Saf, get out of the way," he growled, the sword still raised.

"Nay, Devil, no' yet. Ye said ye trusted me! Ye said we made a good team."

She was making this harder than Merrick could stand. He shook his head, grief and regret churning his stomach. "Ye heard him, Saf! He confessed like this because he *kenned* I would give him a swift death. For betraying his clan and his laird this way, it's the best he can pray for!"

By the bed, Elana let loose a sob, but Gavin said naught. Behind Saf, he planted one fist on the wooden floorboards and leaned forward even further, as if welcoming the blow which would remove his head.

"Merrick," Saf said softer, stepping toward the laird. "He's yer friend."

"And Robbie was my *brother*!"

The words—full of anger and regret and sorrow—were torn from him before he could swallow them back. Robbie had betrayed him, betrayed them all, with his crimes against morality. And now his best friend, whom Merrick had worried about and prayed for, had betrayed the clan.

But Saf understood. With another step, she closed the distance between them, and placed her hand on his chest. "Will ye no' at least hear his reasons?"

It was as if her touch had some sort of magic—and mayhap it did. The rage began to drain from him, coalescing in his chest, right under her hand, and seeping out. His shoulders drooped, and the sword drifted down until it was level with his waist.

"Saf," he whispered, not sure if he liked the way she robbed him of his desire for swift justice.

"Devil, hear him out, aye?"

"And then?" he murmured.

"At least ye'll ken ye have all the information ye need afore making a decision."

She stared up at him. He saw trust and approval there.

Merrick's sigh was half-hearted as he shook his head. "Gavin? My *squire* has bought ye a few moments to explain."

Saf moved out of the way, and Gavin lifted his head. He seemed hesitant, as if unsure what to make of this unaccustomed delay.

"He…" Gavin cleared his throat and straightened from where he leaned against the floor. "He took her, Laird."

"Elana?"

Merrick's gaze darted to where the lass stood, one arm wrapped around her middle, tears streaming down her battered face.

"Aye," Gavin croaked. "Lindsay found her on the road, on her way south weeks ago. He…he took her, and got word to me."

Merrick didn't think he could hate his half-brother more than he did already. He was wrong.

"What did he say to ye?"

Slowly, Gavin climbed to his feet, his movements heavy with dread. "He kenned my position, Laird. He said if I didnae do my best to lead ye astray, to protect his men, he'd…" Gavin cut himself off with a noise which might've been a sob, might've been a growl, but he nodded toward his sister's condition.

Without letting his expression betray his emotions, Merrick silently cursed John Lindsay. The man had robbed his people, destroyed their livelihoods, and now stolen the honor of a good man.

"Was it worth it?" he managed to ask.

His friend, the man he'd trusted, pulled himself to his full height. "To save my sister's life? Aye," he said hoarsely. "I'm yer traitor, Merrick." He shook his head, glanced at his sister, then met Merrick's eyes once more. Gavin spread his arms, hands out. "Elana is watching, Laird. I beg ye to make it quick."

He could dispense justice, aye. But striking down his best friend who was begging for swift mercy? Gavin deserved to die, but his actions had been understandable.

Saf was wrong; finding out all the information had made this decision harder.

"Wait, milord!"

Merrick was saved from making an immediate choice by Elana's outburst. Although Saf tried to stop her, the lass wove her way to her brother's side.

"Elana, nay." Gavin dropped his submissive pose to push her away. "Keep back."

But his sister either didn't care about her safety, or believed Merrick wouldn't strike, because she ducked from her brother's hold and moved to stand before him. The light from her candle illuminated the bruises and blood on her face in chilling detail.

"Laird, he's coming here, tonight."

Merrick's full attention snapped to the girl. "Who?" he barked.

"Lindsay. He's planning to attack tonight. I was supposed to tell ye—" She choked back a sob. "After ye executed Gav, it was my job to make sure ye were warned."

Merrick's throat went dry, and he exchanged a glance with Saf. Gavin had been his second for years. The man knew how he thought. Gavin had come here tonight fully expecting to die for his actions, without even having the chance to explain.

So, he'd prepared his wee sister with the knowledge the Sutherlands needed, to ensure the laird would receive it after his death.

Gavin had been loyal, even going to his death.

"Tell me," Merrick commanded.

So, Gavin explained how Lindsay had made contact originally, messages delivered through a whore in the village, and how he'd received another one that afternoon. He'd been play-acting in the healer's room, frantic with worry over his sister, and wracked with guilt over what he had to do. He'd snuck out and met with Lindsay and his men, who were camped near one of their first attack sites.

"Ye mean," Merrick growled, "when ye led us up the valley, away from the cairn?"

"Aye, that one. He'd brought me Elana's gown, so I kenned he had her. I kenned what he was capable of, Merrick…"

Merrick shook his head, not ready to attempt to understand his feelings on the subject. "Tonight," he snapped in reminder.

"Lindsay had Elana with him tonight. She looked…" Gavin nodded to his sister, who was still silently crying. "I shouldnae have been surprised a bastard like him would break his oath, but I damn near strangled him. I told him I would no longer be his lapdog, and he laughed," Gavin spit out. "The man is half-crazed with greed, Laird. He plans to attack tonight, like a snake, and after he threw Elana to me, he suggested I hide."

But Gavin hadn't. Instead, he'd dragged his sister here to face Merrick, knowing it would mean his death.

It was Saf who asked the important question. "When?"

"The guard change, likely," Gavin supplied. "Lindsay didnae say, but that would make the most sense. His forces match ours, and surprise is on their side. I found Andrew in the great hall and sent him to rouse what warriors he could from the barracks. They'll fight well for ye, Laird. I trained them."

Merrick cursed, his thoughts going in too many directions at once. Anticipation for the coming battle coursed through him as shouts and the sound of steel-on-steel drifted up from the courtyard. Fear for Saf and the bairns mixed with excitement at finally confronting his half-brother.

And Gavin? He was wavering between rage at his friends' betrayal, grief at the man's choice, and awe that the warrior had chosen death over another betrayal. He'd come back to warn them all, even knowing it would mean his head.

His decision made, Merrick darted forward to grab Gavin by the back of the neck. The man moved to guard himself, but halted abruptly as if remembering his choice to submit himself.

Merrick froze, the tip of his blade pressed against his friend's stomach, slicing open the skin but going no further. With his grip on Gavin's neck, it would be a simple matter of pulling the man forward as he thrust it into his gut.

It would not be a clean, nor easy death.

He stared into the eyes of the man he'd trusted.

"If I let ye live, Gavin, will ye betray me again?"

"If ye let me live, Laird," the warrior growled, "I swear I'll spend the rest of my miserable life hunting down that bastard. I'll plant my blade in him, for what he did to Elana."

It was as good a vow as Merrick could expect.

With a swift move, he pushed his second away from him. The man stumbled back, but when Merrick tossed him his sword, managed to catch it.

Ignoring Gavin's confused expression, Merrick whirled to pick up his own sword. "Dinnae let me regret this decision."

Elana threw herself into her brother's arms. "Thank ye, Laird!" she sobbed.

Saf was holding out Merrick's boots when he turned away

from the siblings. "Sounds as if ye'll get the chance to prove yerself, Gavin," she said, obviously listening to the sounds of battle from below.

"Aye," his friend growled as he squeezed his sister once more, then set her away from him. "And when I'm through, someone can tell me what the hell happened since I've been away. Yer squire has *tits*, Merrick."

It was hard to hold onto his grudge, not when battle lust was coursing through his blood. Merrick straightened from pulling on his boots and winked at Saf. "Aye, and fine tits they are."

He whirled and yanked open the door, just as a breathless Andrew tumbled down the hall. "Laird!" he cried, half-falling into the room. "Lindsay is attacking! What is Gavin doing here? Is that Elana?"

Merrick ignored the lad's questions. "Andrew, help Nell and Mary round up the bairns. Elana will show ye wherever Corra and the other kitchen lasses are hiding." He clamped the lad on the shoulder as he steered him toward the nursery. "I'm putting my family's safety in yer hands, lad."

Andrew straightened proudly under his laird's trust. "I'll no' let ye down," he called out as he jogged down the hall.

"Elana, go with them," Gavin commanded as he ran for the stairs down to the great hall.

Merrick would've followed, but there was one thing he needed to do first…

Grabbing Saf's hand, he pulled her into his arms, holding the back of her head as his lips slammed over hers. The kiss was over in far too few heartbeats, and left his blood pounding.

Or mayhap it was the thought of finally facing Lindsay.

"Hide," he commanded as he set her away from him. "I have to ken ye're safe, Saf."

"Nay." She shook her head "Nay, I can help."

"Ye are nae warrior, love," he said gently, in exasperation, already backing away from her. "Keep yerself safe, Saffy. I mean it."

She lifted her fingertips to her lips, still clutching the linen coverlet around her. He nodded and left for the battle.

Lindsay's men were already in the courtyard, and the stables were aflame. Sutherlands swarmed, some panicking to get away, some determined to remove the horses from the fire, some rushing into battle. Shouts and screams and the sound of blades clashing filled the air, which was already hazy with smoke.

Still, when Merrick whirled his sword above his head, he was grinning in anticipation. "Without fear!" he bellowed, knowing his men would recognize the clan rally.

Around him, his warriors took up the cry. "Without fear!"

The Sutherland forces slammed into Lindsay's men.

CHAPTER 13

HIDE?

It was almost a full minute after Merrick had dashed away that Saffy finally shook herself from the daze his kiss had left her in. He wanted her to *hide?*

Well, to hell with that!

She ducked back into his chamber and reached for one of his shirts. She dropped the coverlet around her feet, and as she pulled the linen over her head, she was enveloped in his scent. It took a moment to roll up the sleeves so they didn't dangle over her hands, but there was little she could do for the gaping neckline.

For the first time in a few sennights, she missed her chemise.

Her lips were set in a grim line as she tugged on a pair of Merrick's too-large braies, and yanked hard on the ties. They would have to do.

Hide?

She might not be a warrior, but she wasn't going to hide when she could *help!*

The nursery was near the laird's chambers. Unfortunately,

Nell and Mary were having trouble rousing the sleep-addled children and getting them down the stairs. Andrew was bellowing frantic orders as Mary changed Emma's swaddling, and Maggie was arguing loudly to be allowed to join the fight.

They're the children of my heart.

Merrick hadn't sired this rowdy bunch, but they were most definitely his. And if she was to be his wife—God and Da willing—they'd be the children of *her* heart, as well.

They already were.

Saffy stepped into the room. "Nolan, put down that sweet roll and hold Beck's hand. Do *no'* let him go, ye understand?" She waited for the solid lad to nod before turning to the next pair. "Eva—aye, ye can bring yer dolly—Adelaide is scared, can ye no' see?" The older girl scowled at Saf, but when eight-year-old Eva turned to her, she looked afraid. "Yer sister needs ye to hold her hand, Eva. Can ye follow Elana to the kitchens, and help Adelaide?"

Eva clucked sympathetically and reached for her older sister's hand, Saffy knew she wouldn't get into any trouble on the way. Turning to Maggie, who seemed a combination of excited and afraid, Saffy offered a calming smile.

"Ye're a warrior lass, are ye no'?"

"Aye! But this *clot-heid* says I cannae fight with my father's men!"

She pointed her dagger toward Andrew, causing Mary to frown up at her from where she was finishing up with Emma.

"Andrew is a fine warrior, Maggie, and deserves yer respect."

"He's an ignorant—"

"*Enough!*" bellowed Saf, doing her best impression of Merrick. "Nell, ye have Isobel? Mary, Emma has what she needs?" When both women nodded, Saf gestured to Elana. "Lead the way, please. Andrew, ye scout ahead."

The young man looked irritated she was giving him

instructions, but he nodded in agreement, and slipped out of the room ahead of Gavin's sister, who was no longer crying at least.

As Nell ushered her charges from the room, Saf turned to Maggie once more. "Ye have yer dirk? Do ye have another?"

The twelve-year-old scowled. "Always," she growled, and spun to rifle through a small chest by one of the beds.

She pulled out two more daggers and tossed one to Saf, who caught it gingerly and pulled it from its sheath. She tried to mimic the easy way Maggie stood, brandishing the weapon in front of her, but knew she'd failed when the girl smirked.

"Ye've been training with Da's men, have ye no'? Ye look worse than Adelaide does with a weapon!"

"That's because we're scholars, she and I," Saf snapped in return. But she had to admit the girl was right. While she felt better to be armed, she was no warrior.

As Merrick had said.

With a sigh, she re-sheathed the blade and slipped it into the waist of the braies, hidden by the long tail of Merrick's shirt. At least she wasn't completely defenseless.

"Aright, wee warrior," she said as she nudged Maggie out the door after her siblings. "Ye and I are bringing up the rear. Stay low, dinnae make noise, and have yer dirks ready."

The girl beamed, obviously thrilled to have responsibility. She nodded once and slipped out the door. Saffy breathed a sigh of relief her manipulation had worked, and followed.

The fighting, so far, seemed confined to the courtyard, which was a good thing. It meant the Sutherlands were holding the enemy warriors. She knew Merrick's men were fine fighters, but they'd been taken unaware for the most part. How many had Andrew—thanks to Gavin—been able to rouse from the barracks? How many had been in the village with their families, and now were cut off from the keep's defenses? Was the smoke they could smell from the village, or closer?

Corra and the rest of the kitchen workers were indeed hidden in one of the cellars. Elana helped Andrew lift the heavy hatch and usher everyone down into the darkness. Andrew, taking his responsibility seriously, followed his laird's family into the darkness, and Saf nodded approvingly.

Before she dropped the door again, Mary looked up and met her eyes in the dim light. "Be safe," the lass whispered.

Saf nodded again, although she wasn't sure Merrick's oldest could see her. Mary's concern tugged at her chest, and she wanted to hug the girl. "I—I will. Keep everyone quiet."

"Aye," came the whispered response as the hatch closed once more, trapping the servants and children in the darkness.

Saf spent a moment to offer a prayer for their safety.

If the saints were on their side, Merrick and his men would repel the Lindsay warriors, and the bairns would be released soon, no worse for their midnight adventure.

If Lindsay was successful…

Saf shivered. Well, if John Lindsay was successful in wresting the keep from Merrick, it meant they *all* had problems. He'd take the title of laird.

But that would mean Merrick's death.

This time, Saf shuddered in true fear. The thought of losing him so soon after they'd truly found one another was abhorrent. Yesterday—had it been only yesterday?—when he'd kissed her in front of his clan, his people had shown their support by cheering. When he'd loved her by the waterfall, he'd shown her *his* caring.

And when he'd told her his secret, he'd shown her his trust.

They're the children of my heart.

If she hadn't loved him before, she did at that moment. The Sutherland Devil was a *good man*, and she would not lose him.

Especially not before she had the chance to marry him! She wanted a lifetime doing what they'd done last night… A lifetime playing chess and arguing about clan politics and laughing about their faults and learning from one another.

She wanted to bear his children and love his clan. The Sinclairs were her family, aye, and she'd started on this mission to save her clan. But somewhere along the way, finding the missing jewels had become less important than seeing Merrick as the man he truly was.

She loved him.

Saints preserve us!

Abruptly, the knowledge that Merrick could *die* slammed into her, and Saffy slumped against the door. She could lose Merrick!

Before she truly understood what was happening, her feet had carried her through the great hall and into the armory. The main doors were open, and the noise and smoke from the courtyard was near overpowering.

Pulling the neck of Merrick's shirt up around her nose and mouth, Saf crept slower toward the exit, watching where she placed her bare feet carefully, until she could see the battle.

When she did, she sucked in a gasp so hard she fell to coughing, then gagging on the smoke. Through streaming eyes, she did her best to guess what was happening, whilst doubled-over.

The stables were fully aflame, which explained the screams of horses and men as they did their best to remove the animals. The courtyard swarmed with men wearing colors she recognized from the ambush a sennight ago, and she swallowed thickly when she realized they outnumbered the Sutherlands.

Her throat hurt from the need to cry out, but she couldn't. She might not be a warrior, but she understood enough about tactics to know what was going on.

The Sutherlands were losing.

"Without fear!"

The bellow came from the clump of men where the fighting was thickest, and was picked up by far too few throats.

Saf's cheeks were wet with tears now. She recognized that voice, and understood what it meant when so few answered it.

She was halfway down the steps before a burst of wind swirled through the courtyard, blowing away the smoke long enough for her to see Merrick, his sword flashing in the light from the flames, his face a grim mask.

Merrick!

Had she screamed his name, or just imagined it? Either way, he seemed to hear her.

His blade slashed against the unprotected face of one attacker, and he whirled.

Their eyes met, and she read his lips as much as heard his command.

"Go!"

She shook her head mutely, eyes wide in the face of so much horror and carnage. Leave him? Nay! Her heart would break!

"Saf! Go!"

It was all he yelled before twisting once more to block another sword. He was fighting for his very life, and he'd paused long enough to ensure her safety as best he could.

Saf stumbled backward, her rear end plopping down hard on the steps. In his chambers, he'd said he needed to know she was safe. If he was distracted worrying for her, he wouldn't protect himself as well as he should. And since she couldn't protect him, the wise thing would be to follow his orders and allow him to devote his attention to his own defense.

It was logical, even though it hurt her heart to consider it.

Saf scrambled up the steps to the landing, then flipped over and pushed herself to her feet. She would stay safe, for Merrick and his family.

The doors! They were heavy, aye, but mayhap she could close them, delay the attackers a few precious moments.

It took all her strength to unhook them, but the first swung easily enough. She didn't take the time to appreciate the marvel, however, before rushing for the other side. As she barricaded them, she peered through one of the arrow slits.

Gavin and Merrick were fighting, back to back, moving together the way she'd seen them in training. They were fierce, and somehow graceful, trusting one another to protect them.

Merrick's expression had turned angry. "Lindsay! *Lindsay!*" he was bellowing.

And that's when Saf knew Gavin had been wrong. John Lindsay, despite his promises, had not been leading the attack tonight. He might be here, but he wasn't fighting.

He was the coward Merrick had always thought.

The Lindsay men surged forward, mayhap emboldened by Merrick's cry, and Gavin faced two men at once. He didn't get his sword up quickly enough to block the third, and went down with a blade in his side.

Nausea cramped her stomach, threatening to double her over again, but she forced herself to avert her eyes and breathe through her nose as she barricaded the doors.

If Merrick was going to die in that courtyard, she'd not allow John Lindsay such easy access to the keep.

The bairns and kitchen servants needed to be warned. Choking back her tears, praying frantically, Saf turned and ran.

Even as the roar of battle intensified behind her, she didn't look back.

Couldn't.

Couldn't watch Merrick fall.

A GRUNT ESCAPED Merrick's lips when he was thrown on the rush-covered floor in front of the dais. He'd taken more than a few blows in the last minutes; blows to his body, blows to his soul, and now, blows to his pride.

The blood from the slash which had eventually felled him, spilled from his forehead and into his eyes. He knew from the lightheadedness that he was losing too much blood, too quickly.

Like so many of his clansmen.

"I have waited a long time for this, *brother*."

He'd never met John Lindsay, not in person. But Merrick would've recognized that self-assured sneer. It belonged to a man who had his enemy at his feet and was determined to gloat.

To hell with that.

Merrick grunted again as he got his palms beneath him and pushed. There was a burning in one shoulder, which he refused to allow himself to turn to look at. Either it wasn't bad enough for his attention, or it was. It did not matter; he could do nothing about it now.

Best to concentrate on the coming moments.

He managed to make it as far as his knees before he made the mistake of looking up. His half-brother, clean and untouched by battle, stood on the dais in front of the table where Merrick's family dined. Lindsay sneered down at him, and Merrick imagined how he must look—bloody, filthy, and defeated.

But at least that meant he'd *fought*.

"I should've...known." It was difficult to catch his breath. "Known ye were too much of a coward to face me directly."

Lindsay smirked and stepped from the dais, nodding over Merrick's head. Before he understood what was happening, Merrick's arms were grabbed from behind, his head pulled back so Lindsay didn't have to bend to look him in the face.

"I am facing ye directly now."

Merrick considered spitting, but his mouth was too dry. Gods, had it only been an hour ago he was curled around Saf, secure in the knowledge of their future together?

He'd been…*happy*. Joining with Saf there beside the stream had unlocked something inside of him. Something which had nothing to do with the decade since he'd plunged into a woman, nothing to do with lust.

He'd been *happy* to hold her, happy to tease her, happy to fall asleep with her in his arms. Happy to know his children were safe, and he'd likely planted another one in Saf's womb. Happy that she'd be his wife and her bairn his heir.

God's wounds, but it didn't seem fair!

Fair?

"Life isn't fair, little brother."

Lindsay's sneering announcement jerked Merrick back to the current catastrophe. Had he known Merrick's thoughts? Or was he whining about his own situation?

"I should have been Lord Sutherland," Lindsay was ranting. "My mother was as noble as yours, but *Father* neglected to mention he was already married when he planted me in her belly. This would have been *mine*, and you have been downright cruel to ignore my true claim!"

True claim?

"I had no choice but to attack your—*our* people, you understand. And tonight!" Lindsay whirled, a gleam in his eyes. "Tonight, I have shown you all who *deserves* to be Lord Sutherland! Not *you*, a broken and bleeding loser!"

"Nor ye," Merrick croaked. "A coward who attacks in the night and refuses to face danger."

Lindsay—Merrick refused to think of him as his brother— peered down at him. Then he took two steps forward, pulled back his hand, and slapped Merrick across the mouth so hard, he tasted blood.

Mayhap the blow wouldn't have stung so much had Lindsay's two clansmen not been holding Merrick in place. Of course, if they hadn't been, he wouldn't have knelt there and let Lindsay land the blow.

Darkness began to creep into his vision, but Merrick couldn't shake his head to clear it. He wasn't sure if the dizziness was from the blow or the blood loss. He remembered how weak Saf had been after her wound—a wound from a Lindsay warrior!—and how she'd allowed him to tend to her.

Too bad she'll no' be able to return the favor.

God willing, Saf had followed his order and gotten to safety. He trusted her and Andrew to get the bairns away, to keep them from Lindsay's hands. Even though they were Lindsay's own blood—although somewhat further removed than he suspected—the bastard wouldn't allow any of them to survive to adulthood and challenge his place as laird.

Nay, Saf had to get them to safety.

During the battle, there'd been a moment when he'd turned and sworn he'd seen her on the keep's steps. He'd yelled to her, but the next time he'd whirled in that direction, she'd been gone.

She's safe.

She *had* to be. If he thought she wasn't, there's no way he could accept whatever Lindsay had planned for *him*.

A commotion by the hall drew Lindsay's attention, and Merrick watched from the corner of his eye as two Lindsay warriors dragged a limp man between them.

"What should we do with the traitor, milord?" one asked.

It wasn't until he lifted the limp man's head that Merrick recognized Gavin. Despite his best friend's recent treachery, Merrick had been glad to have him at his back moments before, and although he'd known Gavin had fallen, Merrick's stomach tightened to see him like this.

Gavin had betrayed the Sutherlands, but the Lindsays

seemed to have no loyalty to him either. Dully, Merrick remembered Gav being so sure Saf wasn't a Lindsay. It must've been because he'd known these men. Had he known what they were capable of?

"Is he dead?" Lindsay drawled.

"Nay, milord. We're killing as many of the others as we can, as ye commanded. But the Sutherland bastards are dragging away their wounded before we can reach them."

Merrick surged against his captors then, his heart bleeding to think of his wounded men being cut down like animals. What kind of man issued a command like that? Especially about men who were related to him?

Lindsay ignored his struggles. "Do not worry," he said with a lazy wave. "We will find them later. As long as my brother is dead, they have no one to lead them. Are the fires under control?"

Merrick forced himself to swallow down his pain—and anger at Lindsay's unthinkable command—and listen to his enemies as they described putting out the fires and saving the horses and servants.

"And this one, milord?" the man prompted again.

Lindsay tutted dismissively. "I suppose we cannot kill him, since he did us those small favors, and lent me that delectable sister of his rather against his will. Throw him in the dungeon. Mayhap he will do us a favor and bleed to death."

Merrick watched the men drag Gavin toward the armory and the stone steps down to the dungeon, not sure if he should be thankful his friend still lived. Movement caught his eye, and he watched a small shape flit to the shadows from the door to the kitchens. It floated toward the men holding Gavin, but when they disappeared, the figure stopped and turned toward the dais.

The sun was pinking the eastern sky by now. The attack had come hours before, it seemed, and dawn was heralding a new day. A new day with John Lindsay as the Sutherland Laird, in control of the keep.

Merrick breathed deep, knowing this day would be his last, and trying to be at peace with the knowledge.

Mayhap he would've been, had the growing light not revealed the figure's face.

"Merrick!"

Saf screamed his name as she tore barefoot across the rushes, and he cursed silently. What in damnation did she think she was doing? She couldn't help him, and now he couldn't go to his death knowing she was safe.

Merrick surged forward once more, intent on getting to her, at the same moment, Lindsay lazily reached out and snatched her by her hair, yanking her to a stop.

The warriors behind him forced Merrick to the ground once more, and he met Saf's terrified eyes, willing her not to speak. She was dressed as if she'd just come from bed—*his* bed, and although she wore his clothing, Lindsay couldn't mistake her sex, not with his shirt gaping open on her that way.

She lifted her hands to his, where it gripped her hair, but he merely lifted her off the ground. The noise she made—part whimper, part curse—made Merrick pray for a blade to plant in his half-brother's neck.

Lindsay was peering down at her like she was an inter-esting plaything, and when he licked his lips, Saf shuddered. He turned to grin at Merrick.

"Well, well, brother. Who is this?"

It was that moment that Merrick realized Lindsay hadn't seen his futile attempts to save Saf. All the other man knew was that this wench had screamed Merrick's name and tried to save him.

If Lindsay realized how much she meant to him, the bastard would hurt her just to punish Merrick.

And so, even though it was damn near impossible, Merrick

forced a bland expression as he met his half-brother's eyes. "Just a lass, Lindsay."

The other man hummed thoughtfully and fingered the man's shirt she wore. Saf flinched away from his touch and met Merrick's eyes, the unspoken plea loud in their blue depths.

Forcing himself to harden his heart against her terror, Merrick kept his attention on his half-brother.

"It seems you have a taste for adventurous wenches, brother." Lindsay smirked. "We share that trait, apparently. That Elana was woefully unimpressive—she did naught more than cry when she was under me. I would've slit her throat had I not needed her to keep her brother in line."

Had Lindsay's earlier command to kill the wounded not convinced Merrick he was a monster, his casual admission about raping an unwilling lass did. Bile threatened the back of his throat, but Merrick swallowed.

"Nay, this one…she is weak-willed." Saints, but the lie was hard to utter, made worse by the hurt he saw in her eyes. "She's addled as well." Mayhap, if his lies didn't save her, he could make Lindsay underestimate Saf. "Does little in bed beside cry and pray."

There. That sounded unappealing.

Her tongue flicked out over her lips. "Ye really *are* the Devil, are ye no'?" she hissed at him.

He kept his expression bored as he met her eyes, wondering if the pain he saw was for his words, or if she'd understood what he was trying to do.

Affecting an uninterested shrug, Merrick grunted. She bit out a curse.

But Lindsay was staring down at her, a speculative light in his eyes. "Hm. Mayhap 'tis as my brother says." He leaned down and dragged his tongue across her cheek, making her flinch away once more. "Or mayhap I can make you beg.

When a man's blood lust is high, a wench who just lies there and takes his cock can be appealing as well."

As quick as an adder strike, Lindsay twisted, dragging Saf with him, and tossed her toward one of his men. "Lock her in my new chambers—the laird's chambers. When I'm through with this trash, I'll fuck her black and blue."

Saf's terrified scream mixed with his roar of fury as he threw himself forward once again. This time, his rage lent him enough strength to tear away from one of the warriors. He *needed* to get to her, to save her from this bastard's touch.

He *would*! He wouldn't let her be afraid any longer!

If he had to die to ensure her safety, he refused to allow his last glimpse of her to be the horrified look she threw his way as she was being carried from the hall. He would go to her!

And he would've, had the second warrior not regained his wits and slammed something hard into the back of Merrick's head.

Darkness was all he knew.

CHAPTER 14

THERE WAS no lock on the outside of the laird's chambers, and that took Saffy all of a moment to determine. After the brutish Lindsay warrior threw her into the room, he growled at her to stay put if she knew what was good for her. Was that supposed to intimidate her into staying?

It didn't.

Forcing herself to take deep breaths, she counted slowly to one hundred, then backward just for good measure. Each moment she spent in this room Merrick was a moment closer to death. But she had to be sure there were no guards waiting for her in the hall.

Finally, she cracked the door open to check.

The hall was empty.

Releasing the breath she'd been holding, she pressed her back to the wall beside the door and surveyed what she had available to her.

Assets?

Ye're in Merrick's chambers, which ye ken far better than Lindsay will.

A good point.

Ye're free—despite what Lindsay might think—while Merrick isnae.

A chilling reminder, but which made her more determined to get herself out of this mess and help him.

'Tis possible ye're the only one who can save Merrick and the bairns.

Well, that last one wasn't much of an asset...more of a terror. Leave it to her mind to point it out.

First things first. She crossed directly to the large trunk under the window and levered the lid open.

Although his larger blades, shields, and axes had their places of honor on the walls, this was where the smaller dirks were kept. As his squire, she'd sharpened and polished each one, and knew she could wield them much easier than one of the bigger weapons.

Maggie's small dirk was still tucked into the waist of Merrick's braies she wore, but having a second would be wise.

She'd just started to lower the lid when she heard voices outside, and hurried to stand.

"Make sure my brother is well-secured in the dungeon. I want to save his death until his people are watching. There must be no doubt I am in charge here."

There was a murmur of assent, but Saffy's mind was still focused on Lindsay's words.

Her heart had leapt at the knowledge Merrick was still alive, and knowing what was to come only fortified her resolve.

As the door opened, she backed against the wall beside the small table where she and Merrick had played chess many evenings, and prayed she looked small and terrified.

Actually, the "terror" wasn't that hard to pretend.

Lindsay stomped into the room and seemed surprised to see her. He paused and frowned, then shook his head.

"I am in need of a change of clothes. These are filthy from

riding all evening, but I doubt that Highland brother of mine owns aught but barbarian rags."

He moved toward the washbasin—the water was still cold from the night—and began to wash his hands. Saffy swallowed, eying the distance to the door. Mayhap she could squeeze past with his back turned, since he wasn't yet interested in…what had he said? Fucking her black and blue?

She shivered and swallowed down the bile that threatened to rise. There'd been a moment there, in the hall, when Merrick's eyes had seemed so *hard*, it was possible to believe his words. Possible to believe she meant as little to him as his other women had.

But she'd reminded herself there'd been no other women. Reminded herself that she trusted him, and that he was smart enough to use his wits to manipulate the situation.

And she was smart enough to join him. So, she'd pretended great hurt, and it had nigh broken her heart to see his fear and anger as she'd been dragged out of the room. That, more than her own terror, had been what caused her to cry out so pitifully.

She'd prayed to all the saints in heaven he'd be safe.

When Lindsay turned from the basin, she startled, knowing she'd missed her chance. The knife was pressed against her thigh, and she was glad she'd left the sheath in the chest. With the blade hidden by her body like this, she might be able to strike him if he came close enough.

Unfortunately, she might get her chance.

"I asked you a question, whore," he snapped.

She licked her lips, not bothering to hide her fear, knowing it would help him underestimate her. "I'm—I'm sorry, milord." What had he asked?

"Sutherland's clothing. Does he own aught refined?"

Refined? What kind of question was that? "I dinnae know, milord," she whispered, her voice quavering. Merrick had never worn aught besides his kilt when he was with her, and she had no idea what constituted "refined".

Actually, it was a little ironic that she stood here listening to Lindsay praise Lowlander garb, as it was that which had gotten her tossed into the Sutherland dungeons in the first place.

Mayhap she'd played her part a little too well. Lindsay's eyes raked her, and his gaze turned speculative.

"I only retired here for a wash." He slowly crossed the room, his steps lazy and anticipation in his eyes. "I had, frankly, forgotten all about the little firebrand my brother claimed is meek in bed. But now that I am here..."

He reached down and adjusted his groin, and Saffy's stomach roiled. He was speaking of taking her by force, the same way he'd so casually admitted to raping poor Elana. But Saffy wasn't going to let it happen.

She had her wits, and thanks to Merrick and Citrine's training, she had a blade and knew what to do with it.

Lindsay stopped in front of her, his pupils already dilated with desire, and his breath coming faster. "I wonder, whore, if you will pray and cry when *I* take you?"

Faster than she could understand, he whipped his open palm across her mouth, the same as he'd done to Merrick.

As Saffy jerked backward, slamming into the tapestry-covered wall, he grabbed her by the throat and tossed her toward the bed. She stumbled toward the still-rumpled coverlet, managing to keep the blade hidden under her palm.

She leaned on the mattress with her free hand, trying not to tremble. She could feel the blood leaking from the corner of her mouth, but knew Lindsay hadn't used his full strength on her, as he had on Merrick. Nay, he likely considered that a mere tap, a blow to make her meeker.

Well, it hadn't worked.

She hid her anger and ducked her head as she turned to him, allowing her shoulders to shake as if she were crying.

He was already reaching for the hem of his tunic as he prowled toward the bed. "'Tis best you pray, whore. Whoever you are to my brother, I cannot allow you to live when I'm done with you. I know his reputation for siring bastards, and you're likely already breeding."

Unable to help herself, the corner of her lips tugged up at the thought of already being pregnant with Merrick's baby. She should be terrified by Lindsay's threats, but she was holding a blade, Merrick's trust, and the fate of Merrick's family.

It was impossible not to feel powerful.

So, she lifted her chin and met Lindsay's eyes just as he unbuckled his belt.

Whatever he saw in her gaze, he reared back.

"You *are* a firebrand, are you not?" His chuckle was dry and cruel. "I will enjoy breaking you. Plunging one sword into you afore the final one, so to speak!"

As he laughed at his own joke, she knew the truth. They called Merrick the Sutherland Devil, but true evil stood before her now.

Faster than she could blink, he bit off his laughter and pushed her backward, falling across her and forcing her onto the bed. She began to struggle then, which made him laugh harder.

Half-frantic, feeling his hardness pushing against her thigh as he sought entry to her body, she twisted her grip on the dirk, nicking herself in the process. If only she could turn her forearm, she could plant the blade in his side.

Of course, the throat is the best option.

She stilled, remembering Merrick's lesson from weeks ago. He'd told her the best places to plant her blade...and how to make it happen.

In this position, with Lindsay grunting atop her, she didn't have the leverage she needed. But a well-placed knee to the bollocks...

When her blow landed, Lindsay made an animalistic noise and lurched away from her. It was all the opening she needed to swing her now-free arm up and around, aiming the dirk for his throat.

Her aim might've hit true, except he was still doubled over, one hand cupping his groin and the other trying to hold up his breeches. Her blade, which had been aimed for his vulnerable throat, lodged in his shoulder instead. His roar was half-scream, half-curse, as he reached for the dirk embedded in his flesh.

She didn't stay to see him yank it out, but turned and ran for the door.

Merrick was in the dungeon, and she was his only hope.

AS HE FORCED his eyes open, Merrick couldn't help the groan which escaped his lips.

He knew he was in his own dungeon—the very place where Saf had nearly died, due to Andrew's over-enthusiastic loyalty—and knew there was only one small window. Still, the weak dawn light pierced his dazed brain like some sort of hot blade.

"Merrick? Thank the saints."

The croak came from somewhere to Merrick's left, and it was with great effort that he rolled from his side—where he'd been tossed by Lindsay's men—onto his back to be able to see the speaker.

"Gavin?" he asked in a dry whisper, then winced at how pitiful he sounded.

When the other man lifted his head, he saw it was in fact

his friend. But seeing him dangling in the Lindsays' hold from across the great hall had not prepared Merrick for the sight of Gavin. The other man's face was mottled red and purple already, as bruises rose, with one eye swollen shut and blood seeping from its corner.

"Aye…laird. The bastards…didnae manage…"

Gavin's chest heaved as he struggled to breathe in between his words, and when he trailed off completely, Merrick knew the effort had been too much. He'd seen his friend fall from a wound in his side, and wondered how much blood he had lost from that. Was he even now dying in this cell?

With another groan, Merrick rolled to his opposite side and managed to push himself to his hands and knees. The effort it took required him to stop and rest. His blood pulsed against his temples and the painful spot on his crown, where the blow had landed.

God's wounds, but he was in bad shape!

"I'm sorry, Merrick," came the whisper.

Still on his knees, Merrick turned his head to take in his friend's poor appearance. "Ye fought by my side, Gav." The childhood nickname came easily, as if this was a lark. "And I heard what Lindsay did to Elana. I forgive ye."

Gavin's lips curved weakly upward as he rested his head against the stone behind him. "Thank ye." His breathing sounded a little better in that position. "But I was apologizing for breaking yet another vow to ye."

Merrick grunted in question as he pushed himself to his haunches.

"I…" Gavin closed his eyes. "I didnae kill Lindsay, and I'm afraid I'm no' going to be much use to ye."

Whatever Merrick might've said was lost in a flood of curses as he forced himself to his feet, then stumbled into the wall to hold on until the cell quit spinning.

His friend chuckled dryly. "We're going to die today. I hope ye ken that."

Merrick squeezed his eyes shut and prayed for the world to slow its frantic tilting. "Nay," he croaked. "We will no'. And do ye ken *why?*"

The other man merely grunted.

"Because…" Merrick forced his eyes open, allowing himself to focus on the crude carving directly in front of his face as he braced himself against the cell wall. "Because Saf is up there somewhere, and my bastard of a brother *kens* I love her. I cannae let him hurt her."

It was an easy vow to make, but Merrick had no idea how he'd see it through. He knew for a fact the heavy oak door was barred from the outside, and save for the impossibly high window, there was no other way out…especially not when he felt like this.

But the thought of Saf alone and relying on him sent a surge of strength through him. He pushed away from the stonework, pleased to realize his head had stopped spinning. He forced his eyes to focus on the carvings under his palms, knowing if he could get his brain to cooperate enough to understand the graffiti, he'd be able to think of a way out of this mess.

Graffiti.

His lips twitched.

Saf had been the last person locked in this cell, and she'd sat around and corrected the spelling of the carvings. Here and there, Merrick recognized his grand-uncle's colorful curses, and the more recent carvings atop, pointing out the misspellings.

Even in her darkest hour, Saf hadn't given up. And he wasn't going to give up on her.

"*Her*, eh?" Gavin's breath didn't rattle quite so much when he inhaled. "Ye love her?"

Merrick dragged his dry tongue across his lips and pushed himself away from the wall. "Aye," he said to himself. Then again, stronger: "Aye, I love her. I love her the way I loved Anna. I didnae think to find that again."

"But now that ye have?"

Merrick's palm pressed against the one carved design Saf's corrections hadn't touched, a strange sunburst with a Latin phrase. She hadn't deemed this one worthy of correcting? Or was the spelling fine? Had it been carved by another hand?

His lips felt as if they were cracking. "I'll be marrying her. She's one of the Sinclair Jewels, and her father has already proven willing to align with me."

Gavin whispered an impressed curse under his breath.

"Aye." Merrick grunted as an idea came to him, and he jammed the tips of his fingers into the cracks in the mortar around the sunburst. "'Tis possible she's already carrying my bairn, and this one will be my heir."

"Assuming ye live that long."

The stone pulled away surprisingly easy and without a sound. Frowning, Merrick slid his hand into the opening and wrapped his fingers around a leather sack.

"I'll live," he murmured distractedly as he turned toward the light coming in from the small window. "And what's more, I forbid ye from dying until ye redeem yer sorry arse." He paused in his attempts to untie the pouch to throw a glare at his friend. "And that's the Sutherland Devil telling ye that."

Gavin's lips curved, although his eyes stayed closed and his head back. "Aye, Laird," he drawled. "We'll give that bastard hell."

"Aye, we will. But first…"

Merrick sucked in a breath as he finally got the pouch opened and poured out its contents into his palm. Sparkling up at him was the largest sapphire he'd ever seen, almost the size of his palm, and cut in so many facets it caught and amplified even the weak light.

One of the Sinclair jewels.

Saf had been right.

He felt a lightness bubble up from his chest. It was…hope? Aye, a surety that, with this find, he'd be able to give her what she wanted. He just needed to save her first.

Resolved, he hurried to wrap the stone back up and shoved it back into its hiding spot. When he stooped to recover the brick, he was glad the world didn't tilt. Nay, he was as recovered as he'd get, and he'd save Saf.

"What is that?" came Gavin's croak as Merrick pushed the brick back into place.

He turned, and was pleased to see his friend looking more alert, although his left eye looked as if it'd never recover.

"'Tisnae important, Gav. But do *ye* ken why in all creation the Lewes MacLeod crest would be carved in my dungeon?"

Gavin snorted. "Nay," he rasped. "'Twas it no' yer uncle who spent so much time down here?"

Merrick had already moved toward the door and was examining it for weaknesses. "My father's uncle," he said in distraction as he ran his hands across the oak, hoping for *something* which would allow him an advantage. "And he wasnae a MacLeod. They were barely united then."

Gavin didn't reply, but Merrick had already pushed the mystery to the back of his mind. Restoring the jewels to the Sinclairs was Saf's mission, and if he allowed her to come to harm, the sapphire's location wouldn't matter.

His head jerked around when he heard a noise he didn't recognize from the other side of the door. A scrape, then a thump.

Was someone out there? Someone who was even now pulling the heavy drawbar down, intending to pull the door open?

A friend…or Lindsay?

Merrick motioned for Gavin to stay where he was, although the other man looked half-ready to push himself upright to defend him. Of the two, Merrick was in better shape, so he backed into the center of the cell, planted his weight, and raised his hands, ready to take what was coming.

He didn't expect *Saf*.

When she pulled the door open wide, he didn't think he'd ever seen a more beautiful sight. Her hair was wild, and a bruise was forming on one cheek, but her eyes were bright, and she burst into a smile when she saw him.

"Merrick!" she cried as she threw herself into the cell and his arms.

He did nothing more than wrap himself around her, burying his nose in her hair and inhaling deeply.

She was safe.

She was safe, and she'd come to rescue *him*.

"I love ye," he croaked against her hair. "I love ye, Sapphire Sinclair, and I thought I'd die thinking ye in danger."

Her grin, when she pulled back just enough to meet his eyes, was one of the prettiest things he'd ever seen. "I love ye, too, my Devil, and I kenned I'd couldnae let ye molder down here. Lindsay plans to kill ye today in front of the clan."

"He's welcome to try," Merrick growled.

Now that he had Saf and a chance at freedom, Lindsay would not be standing in his way.

"Where is he?" Gavin asked.

When Saf whirled around, it was obvious from her expression she hadn't noticed the other man slumped against the wall. Or if she had, she'd assumed he was unconscious. She shook her head slightly.

"He's…he's probably no' dead."

That's when Merrick noticed the blood on the sleeve of her —his?—shirt. He lifted her wrist, the shirt falling away to reveal her mostly-healed wound from their last encounter with the Lindsays.

"Is this yer blood?"

She tugged her wrist out of his hand. "Nay, my love. 'Tis his. I remembered what ye taught me about bollocks and throats, but I dinnae think he is dead."

At that moment, they both heard the commotion from outside the cell. It was Lindsay, cursing as he descended the stairs.

"Do ye have a blade now?" Merrick hissed to Saf.

She nodded and pulled out a small dirk from under the tail of her shirt. "Aye. 'Tis Maggie's."

Maggie, his wee warrior. Merrick nodded in approval, and in that moment, knew what had to be done.

"The door. Keep it open, love." He planted a hard kiss on her lips and shoved her toward the opening to their cell. Then he turned to Gavin, who seemed more alert now. "Are ye prepared to redeem yerself, friend?"

Gavin, who'd known him since they were both bairns, understood. "Aye, Laird," he croaked. "And I'll die happy."

"Nay, ye willnae die," Merrick commanded, even as he tossed the sheathed dirk to his friend who sat on his arse to the left of the door.

Gavin rearranged himself so the blade was hidden, then slumped his chin down to his chest so he looked half-dead or asleep.

Just in time, too, because Lindsay barreled into the cell that moment. He was holding his breeches up with one hand, and the other was clasped to his shoulder, where blood was staining his shirt red.

"Where is she? Where is that bitch?"

Merrick thanked all the saints he'd fallen in love with a woman smart enough to hide in the shadows outside. Now, no matter what happened, he knew their exit was secured.

"She's no' here, Lindsay," he growled.

His half-brother seemed crazed, panting as he peered into the corners of the cell, completely dismissing Gavin entirely. "She *is*. I planned to execute you before your clan, but first I'm going to slit that whore's throat. She might already be carrying another one of your bastards, and I have to take care of that brat before I hunt down the rest of them."

The man was standing here threatening his family? Did he not realize Merrick was unfettered?

With a growl, Merrick grabbed his half-brother by the throat and yanked him close until he could stare into the coward's eyes. "Ye willnae face me in battle, but ye developed the bollocks to threaten my family?" He gave Lindsay a little shake for good measure. "There's no warriors to hold me down here, ye bastard."

Lindsay tried to suck in a breath—probably to berate Merrick—but his face was slowly turning purple. And the blood continued to flow from his wound as he weakly scrabbled at Merrick's hold.

Vaguely, Merrick wondered if he could just stand here, waiting for his half-brother to run out of air. It seemed as if his wound was racing to be the thing which killed him, as well. A few more moments of this, and Lindsay would not be any more problem.

And Merrick would've killed another of his brothers.

The thought sent a shudder through him, and he loosened his hold on Lindsay's throat.

God's wounds, what had happened to him? He was the Sutherland Devil, known throughout the Highlands for his swift, decisive justice. He should snap Lindsay's neck and be done with it.

But Saf...she'd been the one to teach him the merit in thinking before he struck. She'd been the one to stand in front of Andrew and Gavin, to urge Merrick to listen to their reasons.

Lindsay had no reasons Merrick could respect—not for rape and murder and betrayal. But still, Merrick hesitated, remembering the feel of Robbie's blood on his hands.

His half-brother was gasping for air, so Merrick changed his hold on the man, yanking him closer once more. "Yer Lindsay family saw ye for what ye were, John. A weak coward who used cruelty to get what he wanted. That's why yer laird uncle has no' given ye any power, aye?"

Gathering what little moisture he could in his mouth, Merrick spat on the bastard. "Ye'll never have the power ye crave. No' at home. And ye'll *never* be the Sutherland."

Lindsay opened his mouth, but with impeccable timing, Gavin chose that moment to bellow *"Without fear!"* and launch himself at Lindsay, dirk bared.

When his friend slammed into them, Merrick stumbled to hold them upright, but needn't have worried.

Gavin was grinning, his eye still grotesque in the dim light, when he straightened and pulled his blade from the base of Lindsay's neck, where he'd sliced the bastard's spine.

As Merrick let his half-brother's body slowly sink to the floor, the two friends stared at one another.

Gavin had kept his vow. Despite his injuries, he seemed more *alive* now than even a few moments before, judging from the way his chest was heaving and he was grinning.

Merrick held out his hand, and his friend gripped his forearm.

"Thank ye."

Thank ye for standing with me. For keeping me from killing another brother. For fulfilling yer vow.

Mayhap Gavin heard all that was unsaid, as he bowed his head in acknowledgement. "For Elana, Laird."

"Aye." Merrick glanced to the open door where Saf was just now peering in. "For love."

Gavin nodded again, then stepped away, and glanced between the two of them, his lips quirked up on one side. "I'll slip through the kitchens to the village, Merrick. With Lindsay gone, his men will be easy to pick off, I think. Give me an hour to rouse what men I can."

"Half at the front gate, then, and bring the other half in through the kitchens. Corra will let them in."

Saf slipped up beside him. "Corra is in one of the cellars with the bairns and Elana."

"I'll stop to alert them then," Gavin said, wiping Maggie's blade on his kilt. "And to thank yer daughter for the loan of her dirk. And to fetch Andrew."

He raised the dagger in salute, then slipped out of the door.

Alone at last—although it was hard to ignore the body slumped at their feet—Merrick pulled Saf into his arms and buried his face against her neck, breathing in the perfect scent of her skin.

"I'm sorry, love. I'm sorry to put ye in this danger." His lips nibbled at her skin. "I'm sorry ye had to see such horrors."

She wriggled against him, tilting her head so he had better access.

"Saf, ye mean so much to me, and I want to spend the rest of our lives keeping ye safe and happy."

"Ye cannae *keep* me safe and happy any more than I can do the same for ye. But mayhap we could work together to—Oh!" She moaned and slipped her arms around his waist. "If ye keep that up, Devil, we might have to start on *the rest of our lives* afore Gavin's reinforcements even arrive!"

Chuckling, Merrick straightened, not even bothering to adjust the bulge under his kilt. Aye, he loved this woman, and aye, there'd likely never be a moment he didn't want to take her to bed. But now was not the time.

"Ye have to promise me, Saf, ye'll be the voice of reason."

"When?"

"*Always.* Ye're smarter than me, I'm realizing. And I—and the Sutherlands—need yer wit and intelligence. Keep me straight, aye?"

Her palm came up to cup his cheek. "I love ye, Merrick. I'll always be there to point out how inappropriate it might be to make love, even if we both want to, because of the body at our feet." Her sapphire eyes bore into his. "And I'll be there to urge ye to think before ye act, so ye dinnae have to be responsible for another brother's death."

It was like she could read his soul. She understood his hesitation when he was holding Lindsay's life in his hands.

Aye, she was right; the time wasn't right for lust. But still, he didn't resist brushing his lips across hers, trying gently to show her what she meant to him.

"I love ye," she sighed.

"And I love, ye." His gaze flicked to the wall with the MacLeod crest. "And since we have a bit of time before Gavin will signal he's ready, I have something to show ye."

Her brows lifted as she followed him to the loose brick. "Aye? I saw this when I was stuck down here, ye ken, but didnae think to examine it."

Merrick pulled free the stone with the carved sunburst and dropped it to the ground. He jerked his chin toward the hole. "Go on."

They were both holding their breath as she removed the leather pouch and poured the sapphire into her hand. When she looked up at him, there were tears in her eyes, and a grin on her lips.

"This is it, Merrick," she whispered. "The second missing stone!"

"Aye," he agreed, gathering her and the stone in his arms. "My Sinclair Jewel."

EPILOGUE

"I'LL BE PLEASED to finally have ye as a son, lad." With a flourish, Saffy's father pressed his seal into the warm wax at the bottom of the contract binding her and Merrick together. "Of course, I need to hear exactly *how* the two of ye came to be betrothed, what with Saffy supposedly staying at the abbey at Dornach all these weeks."

When Da winked at Saffy, a twinkle in his eye, she knew he was teasing her. Moreover, she thought he might have some inkling of where she'd been. Not for the first time, she wondered if Da really *did* know about his daughter's adventures, and was somehow guiding them.

Merrick cleared his throat as he stepped forward to affix his own seal. "I suspect ye and I have much to talk about," he managed with a neutral expression, clearly not entirely at ease with the idea of telling her father she'd seduced him.

But Saffy decided nothing was going to ruin this moment for her, and her grin stretched wide across her face.

She was to be married!

Of course... She dropped her hand to rest on her abdomen.

The way they'd been acting for more than a fortnight, the two of them might as well already be married. She'd stood beside him as they mourned the fallen Sutherlands, worked beside him to rebuild, and eaten at his right hand, helping to wrangle his unruly children. And she slept beside him as well… although they were doing a lot less sleeping than she'd expected.

And although it was still early, she suspected Merrick's potent reputation had already proven true. He'd be a father again in the spring, and once they were married, this babe would be his heir.

Willie had returned from his fostering to help his father, and Saffy had laughed to see the similarities between the two of them. Although the lad was only a half-dozen years younger than her, he seemed so impetuous and hot-headed… and almost as handsome as his sire.

She and Mary had done their best to make Willie's homecoming special, and he seemed to fit in with the rest of Merrick's brood. Saffy smiled, remembering her love's words.

Children of my heart.

Aye, and they'd swiftly become children of her heart as well. Becoming a mother had never been her dream—not like her older sister, Agata—but suddenly acquiring nine children wasn't as hard as she might've imagined. Of course, Mary was more like a sister than a daughter, and if she and Andrew managed to wear down Merrick's resistance soon, they'd be married.

Heavens! Saffy's eyes widened as she realized that Mary could very well make Merrick a grandfather by next year… which would make *her* a grandmother!

She couldn't help it; she burst into giggles, which drew both Merrick and Da's attention. Seeing them together made her heart soar, and her laughter increased. Behind Da, his loyal bodyguard—the Sinclair Hound, otherwise known as Saffy's brother-in-law Gregor—barely twitched a brow.

"Lord help us," Citrine said with a sigh as she moved to Saffy's side to take her arm. "Breeding's made ye addled."

"Breeding?" Da blurted. Then his grin turned wry as he rolled his eyes in Merrick's direction. "I suppose the rumors about yer family are true, eh, Devil?"

"Aye," her love drawled. "And if ye hadnae agreed to an alliance, Sinclair, Saf would still become my wife."

"Ye love her?"

Merrick's nod was quick, certain. "Aye. She's mine. And her bairn will be my heir."

Hearing the words spoken so assuredly—and in front of her father, no less—made Saffy's mood swing from elated to weepy. Her smile turned watery as she met Merrick's gaze.

He blew out an exasperated breath and crossed to her in two quick strides to plant a kiss on her forehead. "I dinnae remember my other women being this emotional."

Even knowing he'd only said it to annoy her, Saffy's mood swung back to irritated in a blink. She jabbed him with a finger. "'Tis because I'm no' yer other women, Devil. I'm special."

He caught her finger in his hand and raised her palm to his lips. "Aye. Ye are."

Her heart melted as he placed a kiss on her sensitive skin, and Citrine sighed loudly beside her.

"I'm stealing her away from ye three louts. I need to visit with my sister!"

Da chuckled and waved his hand in dismissal. "And I need to visit with my auld friend. Have a servant bring up some wine. Sutherland, I think ye remember my Hound?"

Merrick pulled himself to his full height and met Gregor's stare. "*Ye're* the Hound? The one married to Pearl?"

Gregor's chin dropped just slightly in acknowledgement, and when he spoke—a rare event—his voice was a rasp from the injury to his neck so long ago. "I'll no' apologize for taking her from ye, Devil."

Merrick's brow twitched. "I'll no' expect ye to. Saffy tells me the lass is verra much in love with ye. She also tells me ye've changed much since I hanged ye."

When Gregor nodded again, there was *something* in his eyes Saffy hadn't seen before. She knew Gregor was happy in his new life with Pearl, but she wondered how he'd get along with her love.

She wondered if Merrick would admit he'd been wrong to judge Gregor so quickly.

"Duncan is right, then. We have much to discuss." He leaned in closer to the two women. "Go on. Yer father will be safe with me," he assured them in a low voice.

Over the last weeks, Saffy had shared what she knew of her father's condition with Merrick, and he understood how concerned she and her sister were.

They'd arrived at the keep and come right here to Da's solar, so she'd had no chance to speak with Citrine, other than the letter she'd sent soon after Lindsay's defeat. But upon entering the room and seeing Da sitting alone at his desk, looking almost normal…Saffy had burst into tears and hugged him until he'd complained.

Beside her, Citrine nodded to Merrick, then dragged Saffy out into the hall. With their heads tucked together, they walked and whispered just as when they'd been girls.

"He looks so much better, Citrine! Was it just an illness?"

"Nay." Her twin's tone was grim. "I've had him on a bland diet, which he objected most strongly to. No' only does it no' irritate his stomach, it has the benefit of fewer flavorings. I taste everything that goes on his trencher."

Saffy's eyes went wide. "Ye still think it might be poison? Here? In his own keep?"

Her sister shrugged. "A sennight after ye left, he was so bad he couldnae get out of bed. Dougal had to help him with *everything*. But once I changed his diet—and I insisted on being the one to bring him the food—he began to improve. If I'm not able to fetch him his dinner, sometimes he relapses."

"But *ye* haven't had any ill effects?"

Citrine shrugged. "Nay, but I have no' eaten much. If 'tis poison—"

"I cannae believe someone is *poisoning* him, Citrine. It must be a malady. Or something irritating his stomach."

"Mayhap. But I'm no' lessening my guard. Ye'll notice who isnae here?"

Saffy gasped, just as they stepped in their old chambers together. "Dougal?" she hissed. "Ye think Da's *commander* has something to do with this?"

"The man hasnae stopped nagging Da about me marrying that MacLeod lad. He's determined to get me away from the keep."

Saffy blew out an exasperated breath. "That doesnae mean aught beside the fact he wants ye to do what he thinks is yer duty."

"My duty is to my father. *Ye're* the one marrying and giving him grand-bairns."

Citrine poked Saffy in her side, and they both began to chuckle.

"The Sutherland Devil, Saffy! I cannae believe it! I've been out of my mind with worry, not sure if I could send a letter or messenger! And then I got yer letter, and am no' ashamed to admit I cried to hear ye were well. And ye said in yer letter *ye* were the one to stab that bastard Lindsay? I need to hear all about how my training saved the Sutherlands!"

"Well, I *was* Merrick's squire for a while. He gets credit, too."

"I *have* to hear this story!"

Aye, Saffy looked forward to telling her twin everything which had happened in the fortnights since she left the Sinclair holding. Most of all, she needed to talk about Lindsay and the mixture of terror and assurance she'd felt confronting him.

After his death, Gavin had indeed rallied the Sutherland warriors who, along with Merrick's forces inside the keep, had no trouble defeating the leaderless Lindsay men. Enough had died during the initial assault that their numbers were depleted, and less than a score of Sutherland warriors had been lost overall.

It had been a hard-won victory, but the clan was stronger for it. John Lindsay had been defeated, and Merrick had sent an envoy to the Lowland clan to assure the laird his anger had been only for his half-brother. And although there were surely more Sutherland bastards spread throughout the Highlands, no one would dare attempt to replicate Lindsay's claim now that Merrick had been so decisively victorious.

She took a deep breath as Citrine led her toward the window seat. "I have much to tell ye, I believe."

"But first…" Her twin swung her around, placed her hands on Saffy's shoulders, and looked deep into her eyes. "Ye *are* happy? When ye left here, ye acted as if ye were on yer way to yer death."

Saffy chuckled and shook her head. "I almost *was*. Remind me to tell ye about Andrew and my stay in the dungeon. But aye, I'm happy. I love Merrick, and he loves me."

Citrine's firebrand eyes searched her face, as if not quite believing, before she nodded. "I'm glad. I'll miss ye, of course, but I'm glad ye've found happiness, sister."

"Ye will, too, I ken it. One day—"

"Nay," Citrine interrupted, "I'll no' leave Da." Before Saffy could object, her twin released her and made an impatient gesture. "But enough about me. Do ye have *it*?"

There could only be one *it*.

Saffy reached for the pouch she wore on her belt. After so long in breeches, it still felt a little confining to wear skirts. But Merrick had introduced her to all sorts of unexpected benefits that the easy access of skirts provided.

Slightly flushed from the memories, Saffy pulled out the leather pouch and placed it in her sister's palm.

Citrine whistled in appreciation as she slid the huge sapphire from its hiding spot. "Ye found it," she whispered reverently. "This is the second jewel, Saffy." When she met her sister's eyes, Citrine's were bright with excitement. "There should only be two left, aye?"

"Aye. But mayhap if Da kenned we'd found two already…"

Citrine frowned as she tucked the stone away once more and crossed to the small chest she kept under the big bed. "I dinnae ken, Saffy. He's so weak…"

"Mayhap he believes the legend. Did ye ever consider that? If he believes the clan is doomed, mayhap he's already despairing, which is why he tried so hard to get us all married?"

Citrine snorted as she placed the sapphire beside the agate that already resided in the chest, hidden below the ancient tapestry which had started them all down this path.

"He'll no' marry me off so easily," she muttered, closing the lid.

"Mayhap he doesnae need to," Saffy teased. "Da seems quite happy with the matches me and Pearl and Agata have made ourselves."

"And ye think *I'm* likely to find myself a husband?"

Saffy smiled at her twin. "I think ye're likely to do aught ye can to prove ye cannae be controlled."

Citrine burst into laughter as she pushed herself up from

where she'd been squatting and kicked the chest back under the bed. "Ye may be right, sister!"

"I'll tell ye the rest, I promise, but I want to see wee Pearl."

"Aye, and she'll have my skin if I dinnae drag ye out to their little cottage right away. We were right, by the by—she *is* increasing."

Saffy joined her sister in laughter as they moved toward the door. "That news likely helped Da's mood improve, aye?"

"Aye! Ye two will get to race for who births the first grand-bairn."

"And Agata?"

Citrine took her arm even as she shrugged. "She's no' mentioned aught in her letters, aside from how well wee Callan is adjusting. I'm glad she writes so often."

Saffy had just opened her mouth to ask another question about their older sister, when Merrick stepped in the door.

The look in his eyes—part need, part hesitation—made her stop in her tracks.

Citrine looked between the two of them. "I cannae tell if yer meeting with Da and the Hound went well, but I assume I'll learn at dinner."

With a sigh, she wrapped Saffy in a quick hug. "I'll pop out to visit with Pearl and invite her to the keep for the meal. Ye'll promise to make time for me later?"

Saffy wanted to protest, for she'd only just arrived, and would spend all the time with her twin as possible. But she'd learned lately that when Merrick looked at her *that* way, she wasn't able to concentrate on aught else.

"Aye..." she agreed, her gaze on her future husband. She barely heard her sister snort and slip out of their chambers.

When they were alone, Merrick pushed the door closed, without ever taking his eyes off hers.

"Devil?" she asked hesitantly, crossing to him.

Quick as lightning, he reached out and snatched her

against him, his hand going to the back of her head. "He's a good man, Saf."

"Da?"

"The Hound. Gregor. I'm…" He shook his head and closed his eyes. "I should no' have done what I did to him," he admitted, dropping his forehead to hers.

"'Twas more than a decade ago, Merrick," she murmured, her hand snaking around him to rub his back in comfort. "Ye have changed since then."

When he exhaled, his breath mixed with hers. "I've changed even more since ye came into my life, my wee jewel."

"For the better, I hope?" she teased.

When he flexed his hips, she felt his erection beneath his kilt, and the knowledge sent a spike of warmth through her.

"Ye tell me," he growled, his eyes flashing open once more.

She swallowed, arousal pooling in the center of her being. "*Much* better," she managed past a dry throat.

And when she ground her hips against his, the noise he made was part moan, part laugh.

She squealed when he scooped her into his arms and crossed toward the bed. "What are ye doing, Devil?"

"I'm an auld man, Saf. I need to be lying down when I let my wife have her way with me. None of this fucking against doors the way the young ones do it."

She laughed as he tossed her onto the bed, and she hurried to pull her gown up around her waist. He was already reaching under his kilt, and her body hummed in anticipation.

But as he lowered himself onto her, she stopped him with a raised finger.

"What?" he growled.

"Just this once, my love. Then ye must rest up, for I need ye to be in top form."

"For dinner?"

"Nay," she replied with an impish smile. "We've been given

the largest guest chambers, and I want to test the door's—and yer own—strength!"

The sparkle in his striking eyes told her he understood her teasing. Still, his frown was fierce as he leaned in close to her. "Ye think I need to rest up before I can pleasure the woman I love?"

"I think ye have a lifetime to prove it, my Devil!"

AUTHOR'S NOTE
On Historical Accuracy

We've already had the discussion about how 13th-century Scotsmen didn't wear kilts. We decided we didn't care, and were willing to go along—suspension of disbelief and all that—because of the gorgeous model on the cover, right?

So, let's suspend our disbelief a bit more. Just as clan tartans didn't become a *thing* until much later, we can assume clan mottos and crests weren't exactly codified by the 13th Century. But *of course* Merrick and his warriors need a battle cry, so I went with the modern, accepted motto of Clan Sutherland: *Without Fear.*

As for the MacLeod crest, that's a little harder; in the time this story takes place, the MacLeods of Lewes were still a brand-new clan. That will definitely come into the next and final episode in the Sinclair Jewels series, *The MacLeod Pirate.* But in the meantime, we'll just have to pretend the Lewes MacLeods already had their crest in place, and it was well-known enough for Merrick to recognize it when he found it carved on the wall to his dungeon.

How exactly did it get there? And who hid the large sapphire behind it? Will the rest of the jewels be recovered in time, or will Laird Sinclair continue to decline?

Pick up Citrine's story—*The MacLeod Pirate*—to find out!

And seeing as how I completely and utterly fell in love with the chaos at the Sutherland holding, you can darn well bet we'll be re-visiting. Maybe not in the Sinclair Jewels series, but I think Gavin, Elana, and all of Merrick's adorable bairns deserve their own happily ever afters, don't you?

Sign up for my newsletter, follow me on Amazon, or follow me on Bookbub to get the notice when these new series are ready for you!

And as always, happy reading!

From *The MacLeod Pirate!*

The blade changed directions midair, slicing toward her head. Citrine managed to get her short sword up in time to deflect the blow, but the jarring force of the strike left her arms weak.

She spun to the side, flicking her opponent's blade off hers and buying herself a moment's respite to wipe her arm across her brow. The sweat caused her unruly, blonde hair to stick to her forehead, and not for the first time, she lamented the convention which forced her to keep it long.

"Again!" she panted, lifting her sword in the ready position.

William, one of the younger Sinclair warriors, shrugged. "Ye sure, Citrine?"

"Aye! *Again!*"

In response to the command in her tone, William threw himself forward, his blade flashing in the summer afternoon sunlight. She parried one, then two strikes, before he made use of the earlier technique.

She stopped him easier this time. Knowing she couldn't

hold him for long—his arms were stronger than hers, after all—she held up a hand. "Hold."

William immediately stepped back, a smirk on that face she'd once thought handsome. "Had enough?"

Enough? Aye, she was worn down…but not beaten.

Never beaten.

She'd been a young girl when she'd first snuck out to watch her father's men train, and no one had stopped her. That progressed to training on her own, to now, where she trained *with* the men. Her father's commander, Dougal, disapproved, but Da hadn't objected, so the men allowed it.

Still, it was days like today that she wondered why she pushed herself.

Ye could always go practice yer embroidery.

The thought made her snort, a wry grin creeping across her face.

"Show me," she commanded.

The young man's smirk changed to a frown. "What?"

She stifled her sigh. To think she'd once had *feelings* for him! Could she even call William a man? He wasn't much older than her, but he'd proven his worth as a warrior earlier this summer, when he'd been one of the only survivors of an attack on her younger sister, Pearl.

Still, she eyed him derisively. His thin shoulders and slight frame might once have inspired desire in her, but no longer.

The fact he insisted on hiding the wounds he received during that bandit attack by wearing a tunic even during training…well, suffice it to say she was no longer impressed.

"*Show me*," she repeated louder. Settling into position, she gestured him to attack. "Slower this time, so I might learn. 'Tis why I'm here, after all."

From the frown on his face, it was clear he didn't think she should be there at all. "And 'tis my responsibility to teach ye?"

She huffed and rolled her eyes, lifting her sword higher.

"Come now, William. Ye perfect yer own skills by teaching, ye ken that."

When he still looked unconvinced and glanced toward another pair of sparring partners, she tried another tactic. Clearing her throat, she forced a contrite expression. "Please?"

The *please* must've done it, because he sighed and took up position. "*Fine*. I suppose I can do a pretty lass a favor or two."

She might've objected to his meaning if he hadn't *finally* consented to attack her again, and her focus was taken up by studying his moves. After the third round, she was ready to try the move on *him*, and was pleased to see her attack was quick enough to cause him to fumble to raise his hand and block her.

And so they went, back and forth, studying one another for weaknesses to exploit and throwing taunts.

The taunting was a typical part of training among the Sinclair warriors, but most avoided it with Citrine. Only William bothered, and only because of what they'd once shared.

When she'd been younger, she had fancied herself in love with the lad. And whether or not it had been honorable, he'd taken what had been offered. She'd lost her virginity in the stables in a thoroughly unsatisfying encounter. The second and third times had been pleasant enough, but when she'd realized he wasn't at all interested in her pleasure, she'd told him never again.

And mayhap he hadn't forgiven her for that, judging from the bitterness in his eyes as he waited for her to attack once more.

"Have ye learned it, lass?"

She blew out a breath and lifted an eyebrow, refusing to show how exhausted she was. "Ye tell me!"

Her blows landed swift and hard, and she heard him grunt as he stumbled back. The realization she had unbalanced him brought a grim smile to her lips, but she didn't let up on her attack. It wasn't until he cursed and spun out of the way that she let up, but that was a mistake. He only dropped, swiping at her knees.

She almost didn't see the new tactic, although she should've. Exhaustion had stolen her attention and speed, but when she realized the blade was prepared to take out her legs, she leapt…and landed wrong, her left leg buckling.

With a grunt, she went down, rolling, and forcing herself up to her knees.

This was training, aye, but she'd always demanded the men not go easy on her. She wanted to learn, to be valuable to the clan, and she couldn't do that by giving up and staying on the ground when she fell.

Get up.

Another grunt as she shoved one leg under her, only to see William lift his sword in a begrudging salute.

Confused, she lifted her own, albeit slower, and frowned when he moved away. By all the saints, was he conceding? Because she hadn't conceded his win, and what would cause him—

Oh.

Standing to one side of the training area with his arms crossed in front of his still-powerful chest, Laird Duncan Sinclair was frowning at her.

Doing her best to hide her exhaustion, she forced herself to her feet, pulled a rag from her belt, and made a show of wiping down her blade before lovingly sliding it back into the scabbard at her hip.

She used the same rag to wipe her forehead and neck, tucking the stray hairs behind her ears and thinking longingly of the loch's cool water. Then, and only then, did she move toward her father.

"Hello, Da," she called cheerfully as she got closer. "Here to watch me kick William's arse?"

Mayhap it was the right greeting. Almost reluctantly, his scowl eased. "Ye *were* doing quite well. The lad isnae the right partner for ye, though."

Her brows rose as she settled her fists on her hips. As every day, she wore a tunic belted loosely over a pair of trews. Her feet were bare, but her boots lay in the grass up on the hill where she and her sisters used to sit to watch the men train.

"Ye think I need a better partner?" What did Da know of her history with William?

"The lad isnae a bad opponent, but he doesnae challenge ye, Citrine. Ye need a challenge."

She leapt at the opportunity. "So ye're saying I should train with Dougal and the older warriors?" It was a right denied to the youngest among them…and most definitely to the laird's *daughter*.

"Nay, lass." He shook his head almost regretfully. "I'm saying ye need a different kind of challenge. The sword doesnae challenge ye anymore."

With a sinking feeling, Citrine took the waterskin he offered her. "What would?" she asked dully, suspecting she knew the answer.

"Being a wife and mother. Walk with me."

He didn't wait to see if she objected but turned toward the keep. Citrine followed, the waterskin dangling from one hand as she focused on the path ahead of her.

Wife and mother, bah!

At the start of the new year, Da had suddenly begun talking about marriage contracts for his four daughters. Mother had been long gone, and without sons to follow him, Da was obviously concerned with ensuring his daughters' safety.

Pearl—the youngest of Citrine's sisters—had been

betrothed to the Sutherland laird, but had broken that contract to marry Da's longtime bodyguard, the Sinclair Hound. Their oldest sister was now happily married to the Mackenzie regent, and raising the next laird of that clan. And Citrine's twin sister, Saffy, had only just returned to her new home among the Sutherlands, after having joyfully wed Pearl's old suitor.

She was thrilled for her sisters, for certes. They'd all found love where they didn't expect it, and were settled into their new lives as wives and—aye—even mothers.

But not Citrine.

Her place was here by her father's side, ensuring his rule lasted for as long as possible and keeping her clan together.

But a month ago he'd announced her betrothal to the youngest son of one of the MacLeod clans among the Western Isles. Likely a pock-faced lad, too young to piss off a curtain wall, who cared only for the power an alliance with the once-powerful Sinclairs would bring.

"Da, I dinnae want those things," she began, only to have him raise a hand to cut her off.

"Aye, I ken it, Citrine."

With a sigh, he sank down on one of the boulders lining the path, and she realized he'd led her this way to give them a little privacy for their talk. She was normally too full of energy to sit still, but today…

She sat at his feet, her back to the same boulder, and pulled her knees up to wrap her arms around them.

"Citrine, yer mother and I…we wanted ye to be safe." When she started to object, he continued. "And ye're no' safe here, unmarried. Ye ken I'm getting older. The last few months have taught us both that."

Halfway through the summer, Da was laid low by an unexplained stomach ailment. He had grown weaker and weaker, and Citrine had been genuinely afraid she'd lose him.

It wasn't until she began to check his food and ensuring he

only ate what she fed him, that he began to improve. It was enough to go to him with her suspicions.

"The last few months have taught us who to trust," she grumbled.

"I ken ye believe I was being poisoned, and I dinnae deny 'tis a possibility. But I also reject yer theory of my enemy. Dougal is no' only my cousin, but has been my second-in-command for many years."

Throwing up her hands, she blew out an exasperated breath. "And the only one who stands to gain, Da!"

She twisted, staring up at him. "Ye *were* being poisoned, and Dougal—"

"Who do ye think will take over the clan when I'm gone, Citrine?" her father quietly interrupted.

Her mouth snapped shut, unwilling to contemplate such a future.

The Sinclair laird let out a tired sounding breath and scrubbed a hand over his thick beard. "I'm no' ready to die yet, daughter, but ye ken I've long considered the possibilities. Without a son to follow me as laird, what other choices do I have? I have no living brothers, and without the Jewels…"

It took a moment for Citrine to realize he wasn't speaking of her and her sisters. Long called the Sinclair Jewels by the fanciful Highland folk, the four of them had been named for the jewels in the long-missing Sinclair brooch.

That was what her father referred to. Legend had it that the clan's fortune was tied to the jewels, and when it went missing generations ago, the Sinclairs began to lose power. Now, with no sons to take over the clan after him, Duncan Sinclair was obviously convinced his family would fall into obscurity.

But not all hope was lost.

Unbeknown to him, Citrine and her sisters had embarked on a quest to restore not just the jewels, but the clan to honor. After receiving an ancient tapestry from their elderly nurse,

Elspeth, the sisters followed a clue to the Mackenzie keep. Agata's journey there—and her adventure to find love with her new husband, Jaimie—resulted in finding the first missing stone, an agate as big as a man's thumb.

The clue they'd found with the stone led the sisters to the Sutherlands, where scholarly Saffy took it upon herself to don a disguise and become a squire to the most-feared man in the Highlands. Their adventures led to love, as well as finding the missing sapphire under a block in the dungeon carved with the clan crest of the MacLeods of Lewes.

The MacLeods of Lewes…the same clan her father would have her marry into.

But she'd resisted leaving him. Lewes was on the other side of Scotland, and how could she keep Da safe—from threats like Dougal—if she went there?

But if one of the two missing stones—a citrine and pearl—was on Lewes, how could she not?

Mayhap it was time to tell Da about the stones she and her sisters had already collected? Mayhap the knowledge that two of the four missing jewels were tucked in a wooden box under her bed would improve his mood?

Mayhap he wouldn't insist she marry then, but would allow her to merely *visit* Lewes to retrieve whatever stone was there?

"I can hear ye thinking over there, wee one." Da's voice was quiet, almost sorrowful. "I ken ye're trying to come up with a way out of this, but ye cannae. My mind is made up."

Citrine uncorked the waterskin. "About what?" she asked dully, knowing she wouldn't like the answer.

He waited for her to take a drink.

"Ye're going to be married, Citrine. Rory MacLeod is a good lad—strong and brave. His father and I agree he'll be a good match for ye. A *challenge*."

"And my wants no' matter?"

He chuckled. "Yer sisters have thought to run me in circles, Citrine, choosing their own happiness over the clan's."

She frowned. "All of them married good men, making strong alliances. They didnae need ye to force them to marry."

"Aye, they're good lassies, and now I ken they'll be protected when I'm gone."

That was enough. Despite the wobble in her legs from the sparring, Citrine pushed herself up to loom over her father. "Ye're *no'* going anywhere, Da. I'll make sure."

"Lass…" Shaking his head, her father stood, matching her irritation. "I love ye well, but ye're no' more stubborn than I am. Dougal will no' harm me, and I plan to rule here for a while yet."

She stood on her toes until her nose was inches from his. "But I'll no' be here to see it, that's yer plan? I'll be stuck in some castle that stinks of fish, far from here?"

His lips twitch. "We Sinclairs have a proud seafaring and fishing tradition, lass."

Blowing out a frustrated breath, she sank back to her heels. "Ye ken what I mean, Da." Suddenly tired, she felt the fight drain from her. "Ye really are going to do this?" She peeked up at him.

"Dinnae play meek with me, lass. Ye've kenned about this plan for a while. I only postponed it until I was well and could ensure ye *would* leave. Now I ken what to look for—and aye, I swear, I'll watch for poison. I can do that without ye—ye *will* fulfill the terms of the contract."

Thinking about the marriage contract—signed by Da and the MacLeod—she frowned.

"Och, Citrine."

Da clucked his tongue and, after glancing left and right to ensure they were still alone, pulled her into a hug. She didn't *want* to be comforted—she wanted to maintain her anger, to slowly stoke the flames until they burned bright—but feeling her father's arms around her was too much. She hugged him back, burrowing her face in his shoulder.

"Ye're a good daughter. I raised ye to understand honor and sacrifice, like any good warrior. I ken ye'll do what's right for the Sinclair clan."

Blessed Virgin, why did he have to make it sound so *final*?

Setting her back, he placed his hands on her shoulders and nodded firmly. "Think of it this way, lass: 'Twill be a challenge. One ye've never met before. If yer marriage is anything like mine with yer mother, 'twill be the greatest adventure ye ever have."

Greatest adventure? She stopped herself from snorting in derision. *Unlikely.* Marriage to a man who would expect her to wear dresses and embroider and do whatever the hell it was *ladies* did all day…?

It did not sound like an adventure, but… "A challenge," she mumbled, staring at Da's beard.

"Aye, a challenge. Ye'll do fine, Citrine."

Slowly, she shifted her gaze to the distant mountain, knowing if she met his eyes, he'd see the beginnings of her plan there.

A challenge, eh?

Aye, she *would* go to the MacLeod holding on Lewes. She *would* meet this pock-faced lad her father had betrothed her to.

She *would* find the missing jewel the MacLeods had been hiding all these years.

And then she'd come back home.

Alone.

Because her place was here, at her father's side. For the future of the Sinclairs.

———

Ready for the big finale? In order to reach the MacLeod land, Citrine will have to climb into a boat...which will run afoul of The Black Banner, the pirate terror of the North Sea! In a delightful case of mistaken identity, neither will realize the other is actually their betrothed! And when Citrine discovers Rory is in possession of one of the missing jewels... Well, sparks fly! And yes, we definitely get some answers about what's been going on at the Sinclair holding! Check out *The MacLeod Pirate!*

ABOUT THE AUTHOR

USA Today bestselling author Caroline Lee has been reading romance for so long that her fourth-grade teacher used to make her cover her books with paper jackets, but it wasn't until she (mostly) grew up that she realized she could WRITE it too. So she did.

Caroline is living her own little Happily Ever After in NC with her husband, sons, daughter Princess Wiggles. She thinks it's important to note that she made it all the way through grad school (her second history degree) without knowing how to touch-type (she taught herself to type only a few years ago and APPARENTLY lesrned imcorrectly--*learned incorrectly,* a fact which she's only now realizing, as other authors point and laugh). Caroline adores rodents, goes through laptops like Pez, and never met a whisk(e)y she didn't like. She's also pretty funny in person. Promise.

You can find her at www.CarolineLeeRomance.com.

Want the scoop on new books? Join Caroline's Cohort, an exclusive reader group! Or sign up for my mailing list by texting "Caroline" to 42828 to get started!

Hilarious Scottish RomComs:
The Hots for Scots (8 books)
Highlander Ever After (3 books)
Bad in Plaid (6 books)
Second-Chance Manor (2 books)
Those Kilted Bastards (4 books)
Surprise! Dukes (5 books)

Steamy Scottish Historicals:
The Sinclair Jewels (4 books)
The Highland Angels (5 books)

Sensual Historical Westerns:
Black Aces (3 books)
Sunset Valley (3 books)
Everland Ever After (10 books)

The Sweet Cheyenne Quartet (6 books)

Sweet Contemporary Westerns
Quinn Valley Ranch (5 books)
River's End Ranch (14 books)
The Cowboys of Cauldron Valley (7 books)
The Calendar Girls' Ranch (6 books)

Click **here** to find a complete list of Caroline's books.

*Sign up for Caroline's Newsletter to receive exclusive content and freebies, as well as first dibs on her books! Or if newsletters aren't your thing, follow her on **Bookbub** for a quick, concise new release alert every time she publishes a book!*

www.ingramcontent.com/pod-product-compliance
Lightning Source LLC
Chambersburg PA
CBHW061247120726
48001CB00001B/193